Season of Secrets

DANA LEEANN

MELISSA MCSHERRY

Trigger Warnings

YOUR MENTAL HEALTH MATTERS.

Please read the entire list of trigger warnings, then decide if this book is for you. It's fast-paced and dirty, so buckle up.

TRIGGER WARNINGS INCLUDE: explicit sexual content, explicit language, brief stalking tendencies, overly obsessive alpha male, inappropriate use of a hockey stick, inappropriate use of a hockey skate, knife/skate play, unsanitary blood play, choking, spanking, hair pulling, physical fighting between male main character and side characters, meddling family members, blackmail, leaked sex tape, brief sexual assault over clothes, foreign objects used in foreplay

Playlist

Austin Hall - *100 Ways*
Julia - Michaels - *Issues*
Chase Atlantic - *Her*
Nikki Idol - *Sex In Paris*
BOKN - *Dirty Truth*
Chris Grey - *Us Against The World*
DeLyzer, Lilianna Wilde - *Pretty Girls*
Ariana Grande - *Goodnight And Go*
Shaker, COBRA - *In The Dark*
SWIM - *Eyes On You*
Limi - *Cuts*
Always Never - *Bad For Me*

Makos Roster

TEAM

    #60 Duke Lexington - Forward Captain

    #43 Carter Bishop - Forward

    #31 Hawke Hamilton - Defensemen

    #75 Jace Stanley - Defensemen

    #87 Mason Mathers - Defensemen

    #63 Robert Rice - Defensemen

    #12 Nolan Armstrong - Left Winger

    #52 Noah Armstrong - Right Winger

    #90 Grant Stone - Goalie

    #78 Lukas Laine - Goalie

COACHES

    Ken McCoy - Head Coach

    Jake Samson - Assistant Coach

For the puck bunnies who dream of getting railed by the star player in the sin bin.

Sit down, and be a good girl.

Duke Lexington has everything you're craving.

Chapter One

DUKE

"Lexington! We're all heading to Johnny's after showers. You in?" Armstrong shouts from across the locker room. Wiping the sweat from my brow, I can think of a million other places I'd rather be tonight. Practice went smoothly, but my body is killing me and if I'm going to be ready for this season, my aching muscles need proper rest. On the other hand, I know how it will look to the team and the coach if I don't show up.

Tipping my chin up to him, I smirk and reply, "Sure thing, I'll meet you guys there."

Johnny's is the local sports bar. For years, it's been known to be the hangout spot of the NYU Makos hockey team.

My team.

This is my first year with the captain patch, and not showing up to celebrate the start of the season with the guys just wouldn't look right. Image is important, especially when your goal is to make it to the NHL. My entire life has been about hockey and how to ensure I make it to the big leagues. Growing up on the Upper East Side, money was never a problem, and as one could imagine, it meant my parents made sure I was always in the best schools and training camps. They spared no expense. The moment I was old enough to hold a stick in my hand, hockey became my life whether I wanted it to or not.

Don't get me wrong; I love hockey. I live, eat, and breathe the sport, and I share their dream of me making it to the NHL, but that isn't where their control over my future stops. My parents seem to think they need to control *every* aspect of my life because if, heaven forbid, anything messes up their big plans, they'll need multiple backup plans. The fancy car, the designer clothes, and even the friends they forced on me as a child have all pushed me further into the public eye and into the right crowds to get me where I am today. Am I thankful? Sure, but I'm also resentful. Part of me feels like they didn't think I was good enough to get where I am on skill alone, and to be honest, that shit hurts.

It hurts about as much as my constant getting into shit and fighting hurts my parents.

"Duke seems to be showing signs of violent tendencies."

That's what the social worker told my parents the last time. She's not wrong. I'm only human, and holding in my feelings takes its toll. Eventually, I snap just like everyone else. More often than most, apparently, but hey, I can't be good at everything.

Their doubt in me is the fuel to my aggression. Well, part of it. The rest of it comes from Olivia, the girl my parents set me up with in our freshman year at NYU because her family was "up to their standards" and had an abundance of money. The same Olivia who ended up fucking my best friend and breaking my heart less than six months later. We're still together, in the public eye anyway, because ending it meant not only letting my parents down yet again but also pissing off my coach, who just so happens to be Liv's dad.

Liv keeps our arrangement between us, but she doesn't like it. She's made it clear she wants me back and is convinced I'll come crawling back to her in time. Not a chance. I draw the line at cheating and lying, but I'm willing to pretend if it keeps me on the roster and my parents off my back.

Packing away my gear, I grab my body wash along with the white towel from the metal hook in my locker and then head to the shower stalls at the back of the locker room. Most of the team has already taken off, including my best friend Hawke Hamilton, the best left winger in our league. Knowing him, he dipped out early with

Nolan Armstrong, eager to get the first dibs on the puck bunnies that surely await our arrival. Reaching one of the empty stalls, I step inside, not bothering to close the curtain behind me, and place my body wash on the wall beside me before I turn on the faucet. A hiss slips from my lips as streams of ice-cold water cascade down my body for a few brief seconds before it warms up and finally hits the scalding temperature I love. Closing my eyes, I step under the water, running my hands through my dark hair as it rushes over me.

"Are you kidding me?" The echoing shout from one of the guys hits my ears. Snapping my eyes open, I watch as Grant Stone rushes towards the showers in nothing more than a pair of Calvin Klein briefs with his phone in his hand. His blonde shoulder-length hair is still slick and sticking to his neck and shoulders as he saunters in.

"What the fuck are you on about, Stone?" Stanley, our defenseman, laughs from a few shower stalls down.

"The Knights are at Johnny's, man. Tell me that's not some slap-to-the-face shit," Stone snaps. Grabbing my bottle of Old Spice body wash, I squirt some into my hand before rubbing my hands along my skin, spreading the lather around my body.

The Boston University Knights.

Normally, I wouldn't give a fuck about them being in our side of town, let alone our spot. But this year, they're being led by my childhood rival. Ace Anderson. I have no doubt this little visit to Johnny's is his way of stirring the pot, testing the waters to see if he can get me to blow up and get me kicked from a few games.

"You're joking, right?" Stanley laughs. "Well, looks like their new captain has more balls than the last one then, eh?"

"No. It's all over Twitter, man. They have to know we're going to show up there, right? I mean, Johnny's is Makos territory." It's clear from the tone of Stone's voice he isn't happy.

Stone is the pitbull of the team. He's a young freshman, eager to prove to us and the coach that he deserves to be here. What he hasn't figured out is we already know he does. I've yet to see a puck make its way past him and reach Stanley. The kid is talented as fuck.

Letting my head fall back, I stand beneath the water, rinsing the suds from my body.

"Oh for sure. They're probably counting on it, but the question is, how are we gonna respond?" Jace asks. Without even opening my eyes, I know the question is directed at me.

Being captain means that the team follows me, and though it should only be on the ice, the respect and brotherhood the guys and I have built translates off the ice as well. No one will react to the Knights being at Johnny's unless I say so. No matter how badly they want to. Luckily for them, if there's one thing I've grown to love over the years besides hockey, it's fucking with Ace Anderson and his plans.

"I think the real question is, boys, are you ready to go hunting?" I respond.

"Fuck yeah!" Stone shouts, slamming his hand down on one of the rusty red steel lockers.

"We're going to show them how Makos greets unwanted fish in our waters," I add as I turn the shower faucet off. Grabbing the towel from the ledge, I wrap it around my waist and head toward my locker. I guess how I'm spending the night has been decided for me. There's no way I'm missing out on a chance to mess with Ace, especially when he's the one who came here looking for it. Knights don't belong in Makos territory, and the fucker knows it, but I'm happy to play his little game.

The guys head out one by one, knocking their knuckles against mine as they pass by me. Alone, the locker room is so quiet and empty that every sound echoes, including the sound of my bag as I zip it up before throwing it over my shoulder. I take one last look at my jersey with the captain's patch hanging in my locker before slamming the door closed and making my way out of the locker room.

"Jesus, what took you so long?" Liv snaps with an impatient tone as she pushes off the wall and makes her way toward me.

Fuck.

Just when I thought I could get away without having to see her face tonight.

"What are you doing here, Liv?" I reply in a hushed tone. She wraps her arms around my neck and pulls me in for a kiss. The scent of expensive perfume is so thick, and the moment she presses her botox-injected lips against mine, I wanna puke. Don't get me wrong, Liv is good-looking, but nothing about her is real, except the brand name shit she parades around in, like it makes her a fucking goddess that everyone should bow down to. I was naive enough to fall for her facade, but that shit was a long time ago. Now, I see her for what she is.

Pulling back, I head out of the arena and towards my car. "What kind of question is that? Obviously, I'm going to Johnny's with you, Duke," she adds demandingly as she struggles to keep up with her Louis Vuitton heels on. No doubt the news of the Knights being at Johnny's has spread, and Liv may be an idiot, but even she knows that as captain, I can't *not* show up—not with rivals in our spot. "You know Daddy would just ask questions if you showed up without me."

"He isn't even going to be there. It's just me and the guys, and quite frankly, it's already going to be a shit show, and I'd rather not have to keep up with your bullshit, too."

"Wow, Duke, I'm offended. Is this really how you're going to speak to me? Your girlfriend?" She scoffs, hooking her arms around mine as I drag her beside me. "Besides, he already knows I'm going with you, obviously. Otherwise, I'd have gotten a ride home with him after practice. You looked good out there today."

"Don't pretend to give a shit about how I look on the ice, Olivia. And for the last time, you're not my fucking girlfriend. You mean fuck all to me, and you know it."

"Oh, come on, Duke." She stops, pausing in the middle of the dark parking lot. "You can't hate me forever. I made one mistake, okay? One. I'm not fucking perfect, and neither are you!" she shouts.

I roll my eyes as I pop open the trunk of my 2023 matte black Lexus 300 F, then toss my bag and stick inside before slamming it closed. We've had this argument a million times already, and while I agree that neither of us is perfect, there's no excuse for the hurt she caused me. No excuse for lying or cheating.

"Jesus, Liv. Will you give it up already? I don't fucking care. You did what you did, and we're done."

"Yeah, right. Everywhere except the public eye, though, right? Cause you need me, and you know it. How long will Daddy let you keep that captain's patch once he finds out you broke his precious baby girl's heart, hmm?" she hisses as she brings herself to stand before me. I look down on her as she runs her fake nail across my chest, but I push her away. I know she's right, and I don't fucking like it.

My jaw clicks with anger. "Get in the fucking car and shut up," I reply through tightly clenched teeth. She smirks, content in knowing she fucking won, yet again. She always does.

Liv does as she's told and climbs into the passenger seat. Leaning against the trunk, my head falls back, and my eyes find their way to the deep blue night sky. It's clear, and the cool fall air is crisp. I'm stuck. As much as I hate this arrangement we have, I can't do a fucking thing about it. What I can do is direct my frustrations at Ace and his little gang of Knights that seem to have found their way into Makos waters.

Climbing into my car, I start it up and rev the engine before pulling out of the lot and heading to Johnny's.

Let's get this shit over with.

Chapter Two

ASPEN

School, work, hockey.

Repeat.

Again and again until I'm chewed up and spit out on the other side of hockey season, unsure of who I am or what day it is. The chaos doesn't end with hockey season. It slows down just enough for me to feel like I'm finally beginning to catch up, and then the carpet is ripped out from under me when pre-season practices start back up.

I fell into this cycle the day I turned sixteen. The local animal clinic brought me on as a volunteer as soon as I was old enough to drive myself there, and as a result, most of my free time was spent volunteering, learning the ins and outs of the clinic in preparation for my lifelong goal, to be a veterinarian. Nowadays, I work at the clinic as a vet tech while attending the vet-med program at New York University.

My older brother, Ace, has spent the majority of his life slapping a hockey puck around on the ice, so naturally, my childhood was spent doing homework at hockey tournaments while my dad coached my brother's teams. He's the head coach of the Boston University Knights, and it's no surprise my big brother landed himself in the captain's seat once he was old enough.

The NYU hockey team is my brother's biggest competitor, and he's constantly giving me shit for choosing *here* of all places to attend college. I'm in my third year now, and I've finally broken free of dorm life.

"We need to go out and celebrate our newfound freedom! No more dorm advisors, no more rules, and no more sneaking around with the guys we bring home. I don't know about you, but I'd like to break in the rental this evening, if you know what I mean," Ashley says, nonchalantly raising an eyebrow as she watches me unpack a box full of clothes.

Glancing up at her while continuing to remove clothes from the box, I give her a once-over, assessing how serious she is, but I already know she's probably dead set on bringing home another hockey player tonight. She's *obsessed* with the hockey player persona, relentlessly chasing and fucking them because that's her kink. Most of the teams recognize her by now, and she's a well-known puck bunny amongst the players, but she's my best friend. We've been friends for as long as I can remember, and we've done just about everything together. She sleeps around with hockey players and I'm more tightly bound, so we balance each other out perfectly.

One positive of moving out of the dorms is that I have my own bedroom now, and I won't be locked out of my dorm every time she sneaks someone new in for a few hours of fucking. I can actually hide in my room and focus on the hours of homework I need to complete.

"I'd rather stay home and unpack tonight. I have a lot of schoolwork to get done later this week, and I really need to get this done instead of putting it off like I know *you're* going to do. If I don't unpack now, I'll never get around to it."

Ashley scoffs, rolling her eyes. "We both know that's not true. You're too type-A to let it sit for more than a day or two. You'll find the time, trust me," she smiles, clasping her hands together as she bends at the knees. "*Please* come with me tonight. We need to get out and have some fun, and I just heard about a bar where a few of the local teams hang out... I heard the Knights *and* the Makos will be there. I don't know, maybe there'll be a fight tonight. We can't miss it, Aspen!"

Of course, she'd want to go where the Knights are. She's been obsessed with fucking every member of my brother's team since he joined. Some days I'm worried she'll go as far as sleeping with my brother, but I try to shake the thought away, knowing she's a better friend than that.

She may have an unhealthy obsession with hockey players, but she wouldn't fuck her best friend's brother, right?

"You think I want to go drinking where we already know my brother will be?" I laugh, neatly folding the last pair of jeans from the box.

"Pints of the cheap beer are half off today."

That piques my interest, and I don't hesitate in my response. "Sold."

She's silent for a moment, caught off guard. She hadn't expected it would be so easy to persuade me, but she knows how much I like a good sale, especially on beer. I may come from a little bit of money, but my parents didn't build their wealth by recklessly spending it. I've picked up on their habits over the years. I'm even more frugal than they are, but I can't pass up a cold, discounted beer after a long day of moving.

"I'll get my bag," she squeals once she comes out of shock.

"I'm only going for a couple of beers, then you need to leave me alone for the rest of the week and let me study. I can't loosen up on school now just because we're in our own place."

"Yeah, sure," she says, skipping away in search of her bag. "Brynne!!"

Brynne answers her from across the house, yelling back at her. "WHAT?"

"We're going out tonight!" Ashley beams, announcing the news to our roommate.

We met Brynne freshman year and have been friends ever since. She was the missing piece of our trio, creating a balance that we didn't know we needed. Ashley and I are two *very* different extremes, and Brynne falls somewhere in the middle. She's good at mediating when Ashley and I are too far off from one another.

"Is Aspen coming?" Brynne asks with a hint of disbelief in her voice.

"Yes!" I holler through the doorway, joining in on the conversation. "Just this once!"

"We all know that's a lie," Ashley says, returning to my room with her bag thrown over her shoulder. "Change into something else, then we're leaving."

I look down, furrowing my eyebrows as I survey my attire. "What's wrong with this?"

"You look like you just walked out of the gym," Brynne laughs as she enters my room.

"We were moving all day, and *someone* had to do the heavy lifting around here. What do you expect?"

There are sweat stains under the armpits of my shirt and I can smell the body odor coming off of myself, but it isn't anything some perfume and a new shirt can't fix. She's being dramatic.

"Just go change and freshen up a little." Ashley pushes me toward the bathroom, then begins rifling through my neatly folded clothes. "Here," she says, holding up a tightly fitting pair of jeans and a baby-blue top with a low-cut front. "This is perfect."

"Okay," I sigh, rolling my eyes as I take them from her.

I change quickly, slipping into the clothes before I have the desire to change my mind. The jeans cup my ass nicely, showing off my curves in the most flattering way. I brush through my long blonde hair, untangling a few knots before throwing on a little bit of makeup. I don't normally wear many cosmetics. I have a quick five-minute routine I've stuck with for years, and it's never done me wrong.

"Ready," I say as I exit the bathroom, finding my roommates waiting for me on my bed.

"Let's get fucked up," Brynne says as she jumps to her feet.

Ashley's voice is quiet as she mumbles through a laugh, "Or get fucked."

"Or that," I add, making all of us laugh. "I'd rather stick to beer tonight. You do you, though."

The three of us walk out the door together, laughing and chatting as we head toward a bar full of horny hockey players.

Chapter Three

DUKE

Johnny's is packed. The tiny sports bar is usually pretty busy, but tonight it feels like it's unusually full. The music is bumping for a Thursday, and although it's still early, it seems most people are already hammered off their asses. Stone, Rice, and I snag chairs at a table away from the crowds of people while Stanley and Bishop roam the room and chat up some puck bunnies.

Of course, Liv wastes no time plopping her ass on my lap the moment I sit down. Heaven forbid she leaves any other girl the opportunity to approach me.

"Well, well, I was wondering when you boys would make your way in," Johnny chuckles as he wipes his hands on a white towel. I'm assuming you heard about our out-of-town visitors, then, eh?" His salt and pepper beard is pulled into its usual thin braid down his chin, and as a former Makos himself, he's repping with his old vintage team t-shirt.

"More like *unwanted* visitors," Stone chimes in, visibly annoyed.

"It's just beer tonight, Johnny. Clearly, some of the guys are pretty rowdy. Let's not add liquor to that," I laugh, elbowing Stone playfully. His eyes are fixated on the back of the small bar, no doubt where Ace and the BU Knights are posted up.

"And you, sweetheart?" he asks Olivia.

"Just a water for me, please, John. I have places to be tonight," she adds dismissively.

This is one of the many things I hate about Liv and everything her lifestyle represents: looking down on those who aren't "*up to their level*" as they say. My parents are the same way. They treat anyone who isn't from money or a good family like the dirt on their shoes.

"Sounds like a plan. The missus wants me home at a decent hour tonight, so I'd rather not have to stay late cleaning up after another one of your brawls," Johnny adds as he grabs us some beers from the fridge behind him.

"Look at them, just chumming the water. Calling us to dinner like we won't come to play," Stone spits as Johnny hands him his beer.

"That's what you think?" Rice laughs, bringing his

beer to his lips. "They knew what would happen by coming here. Ain't that right, Duke."

"What does it matter why they came?" Liv asks as she applies another layer of gloss to her lips.

"What the fuck does that mean?" Stone snaps, turning his eyes on Liv. She scoffs, tucking her gloss back into her purse and fixing her thick blonde hair before lifting her eyes to his.

"It means they knew what they were doing by coming here—to Makos territory. They're trying to get a rise out of all of you. There's no doubt in my mind that this was Ace's master plan and his way of getting a rise out of Duke. But we're not going to—"

Rice bursts out laughing. "Liv, shut up and let the boys talk. You don't know shit, so stop acting like you do," he adds, cutting her off.

He's not a fan of her. Never has been, and truthfully, most of the guys aren't. They just kiss ass when the coach is around. Usually, they're respectful enough, seeing as they all think she's my girlfriend, but even I don't stop them from telling her off. Why would I?

He continues, "Ain't no way they're coming in here and walking out without getting at least a warning, right, Duke?"

Slowly, I cock my head to the side, taking my first peek at the back of the bar. Ace and his goons are posted up in the bar that usually is filled with Makos. His eyes are already fixated on mine, with a cocky grin plastered on his face. Shit head. The moment I see him, I have the uncontrollable urge to slam my fist into his stupid face. He's leaning back in my usual spot, his arms resting across the back of the chair beside him.

The bar is filled with his teammates and the occasional desperate puck bunny. But one of them stands out—a petite blonde sitting directly beside him as she chats with her two friends on the other side of her.

I lift my beer to my lips, taking a sip while I keep my focus on *her*. Behind me, I can hear Stone and Rice continuing to bitch about the Knights. I can't tell if Stone is more worried about the loss of easy pussy or the fact that I haven't acted on them being here yet. The blonde turns and whispers something in Ace's ear before turning back to her friends. She's cute. Her long, ashy hair hangs around her face, and her makeup is light. Simple. I like that she's not trying to hide her natural beauty behind pounds of makeup like most girls.

Fuck. What is a gem like her doing with a douche like Ace?

"Can we go now? I mean, clearly, this was a waste of time. There's no point in making a scene, and I have shit to do," Liv whispers against my ear.

"Go, then. No one is stopping you. I didn't even want you to come, remember?" I laugh, bringing the beer to my lips again. The bitter liquid glides down my throat until it's gone, and I slam the bottle on the bar. "Johnny, I'll take another."

"Another for me, too," Stone adds.

Nodding, Johnny opens the fridge door and pulls down the amber bottles. "Coming right up."

Though the blonde across the bar has my attention, I can feel Olivia's eyes burning their way into my skull. She might not be my girlfriend, but she is still one hell of a jealous cunt. The blonde and her friends are laughing while looking around the bar. I watch, unable to tear my eyes from her as they scope out the guys, chatting amongst themselves about their options. One in particular seems to have caught the blonde's eye and I watch as she eye fucks him from across the bar.

What the fuck.

My eyes snap to the guy who has caught her attention, and my blood boils. He's a regular here, but other than that, a nobody. Turning my eyes back to her, my anger only grows when I find her flirting with him. The blue top she wore tonight shows off just the right amount of cleavage from her perky little tits and she knows how to use it.

As if sensing me watching, her eyes move from him to me. Instantly, my pulse increases.

Goddamn.

They're not the typical blue you see in someone's

eyes. No. Hers are dark and deep, like the ocean. *Stunning.*

Add the light dusting of freckles across her nose and cheeks, and she is easily the most beautiful woman I've ever seen. The corner of my mouth turns up in a slight smile as I watch. But who the fuck is she? Johnny places my beer on the table next to me, but when I try to grab it, Liv snatches it up. Annoyed with her bullshit, I tear my eyes from the blonde and grab it from her hands.

"You know, it's rude to gawk at other girls when your girlfriend is present," she snaps, clearly annoyed that she's lost my attention. "Besides, there's nothing special about her. I mean, just look at her," she laughs. "She probably picked up that tacky little number from the local Target on her way over here."

"Weren't you leaving?" I retort as I shove her off my lap and turn myself toward the bar. I'm not stupid. She's in a rush to get out of here to go meet up with whatever poor dude she's messing with this week. She'll never admit it, but I'm not the naive guy I once was.

"Oop, seems there's trouble in paradise, Rice," Stone laughs.

"Oh no, whatever shall we do?" Rice is sarcastic, placing his hand over his heart as though he's been injured.

"Fine," she adds, snatching her purse off the bar. "But just so you know, your attitude tonight fucking sucks."

Liv flips her hair and slides her Versace coat over her shoulders before heading out.

Fucking *finally*.

"I don't know why you put up with her shit when there are so many other chicks desperate for a piece of you," Rice smirks, lifting his beer to his lips as he swipes on his cell.

"She probably gives epic head. She *has* to," Stone adds, stretching his arms over his head. "Don't get me wrong, Duke. I love a good blowy as much as any guy, but if it meant I had to deal with *her*? Fucking no thanks."

I laugh, lifting my bottle to my lips again while my eyes make their way back to the blonde that has me puzzled. I've never seen her around, that much I am sure of. I'd remember her. The fact that she's sticking with her friends and not hanging off one of the many hockey players here tonight tells me she's not a puck bunny.

So who the fuck is she, and why is a girl as hot as her with the fucking Knights?

"Ah! She's a hot little thing, ain't she? Waste. It's a shame, really. If she weren't the fucking enemy, I'd fuck her so goddamn good," Stone comments, nodding his head in the direction of the blonde.

Enemy?

"Fuck off, Stone," Rice bursts out laughing. "Aspen fucking Anderson would never give you the time of day, even if she wasn't of Knight blood."

"Anderson?" No way this chick is related to fucking Ace, there's just no way.

"Yep, that right there is Ace Anderson's baby sister. The prettiest piece of off-limits ass on campus," Stone replies, running his tongue across his lips as he watches her.

Risking a glance, I find her laughing at the bar with her friends as she tosses back another drink.

Fuck.

"On campus? She goes to NYU?" I question.

"Yep," he adds. "She's a junior, just started this semester, and no doubt visiting her is what Ace is using as an excuse to hang out in Makos territory. If he thinks we're going to welcome Knights in our waters with open arms just because his sister goes here, he's in for a shock. I'll fuck that bitch right in front of him to prove a point."

"The fuck you will!" I snap unintentionally. Shocked, Rice looks at me confused.

"Oh shit. Our boy has it bad," Stone laughs, slamming his hand down on my shoulder. "Listen, Cap, I have all the respect in the world for you. You know that. You're my homie. But Knight pussy is off-limits, even to you," he adds. "Besides, I don't think Liv would approve. That bitch is a psycho."

I don't give a fuck what Liv thinks, but they don't know that, and they can't. It's in everyone's best interest if they all think that Liv and I are an item. Ignoring his comment, I bring the bottle to my lips and guzzle down the last of my beer while I watch her.

She's so focused. Completely unaware and unbothered by the chaos around her, and *fuck*, she is beautiful. Knight or not, I know this can't be the last time I see her.

"Okay, but serious talk, can you imagine Ace's expression if one of us boned his baby sis?" Stone howls.

"None of us are going to fucking touch her, Stone. Drop it," I spit. For whatever reason, the thought of any of them talking to her infuriates me. I don't want any of them or the team drama around her.

"Jeez, chill man, I was just joking around."

Placing the empty bottle down, I reach into my pocket and pull out a fifty, tossing it on the bar. "Another round, Johnny."

"Ah shit, Cap treating us tonight, huh," Rice smirks cockily. "What are you sucking up for?"

"Sucking up? More like trying to shut you both up so I can actually enjoy my beer before I dip out," I laugh as I run my hand through my hair.

"What? You're kidding, right? They're still here, bro! We're not gonna do shit?" Rice shouts, drawing attention from the people around us.

I know he's pissed, and I get it. It's taking everything in me to walk away. To not go over there and beat the fuck out of Ace and his fucking goons. But I won't. Not with her there. Why? I have no fucking idea, but something in me just knows she doesn't deserve that shit, and I don't want her to see me like that.

I don't want her to see that side of me. The dark side.

"Not tonight. Fuck it, let them think they won. We have other ways of reminding them how friendly Makos can be, and we don't need an audience to do it," I reply, hoping the threat alone will keep the guys happy enough.

"Facts. You're right, Cap. Let them think they won. Then, when we retaliate, they won't see it coming," Stone chirps as he hops around from one foot to the other excitedly. He's feeling the buzz from the beers. "This is why you're the leader, man. Fucking smart," he adds, tapping his finger on the side of his head.

Smirking, I stand up, shaking my head at his bullshit.

"I gotta piss, watch my chair," I reply, before making my way toward the bathrooms.

As I pass the bar where Aspen and her friends are sitting, I notice a guy making his way toward them, and I immediately don't fucking like it.

But I can't show it.

Chapter Four

ASPEN

I'm *actually* enjoying myself. Way more than I thought I would in a bar full of hockey players.

These guys have always been forbidden to me, prohibited by both my father and brother because they know how hockey players treat women. Many of them jump from puck bunny to puck bunny, never having the time, energy, or the will to stick to one woman.

Ashley and Brynne are buzzed, swaying more toward the drunk side. They're laughing and giggling, which in turn is making me smile and loosen up for the first time in weeks. The cheap beer is flowing from the tap, and we're drinking it as quickly as it comes.

We ran into my brother as soon as we walked in, and he's pissed. He's hovering around me with a few of his friends, making sure none of these hockey players approach me, which is beginning to annoy the girls because that's the main reason they're here. To be honest, it's frustrating me as well. I'm having a good time, carefree and innocent, and he feels the need to be overprotective and possessive. I can't say this is a new behavior for him, though. He's always been this way.

"Don't you have anything better to do, Ace?" Brynne finally asks my brother, eyeing him as she guzzles down another mug of beer. She sets it down when it's empty, then glances around the room, throwing her hand up as she points. "Do you see all of these beautiful girls here? I'm sure more than one of them would like to go home with the captain of the Knights."

Ace looks around, flicking his blue eyes between the women. I watch his shaggy blonde hair sway as he surveys the girls. There's conflict on his face, but I think he's seriously considering leaving me alone, so I encourage him.

"I'm a big girl," I sigh, rotating toward him. "I can take care of myself, you know."

Ace turns his attention back to me, and he's silent for a few seconds as he thinks through my words. "I don't like seeing you in a bar full of hockey players," he admits.

"I know," I nod. "But I can make my own decisions. I'm only here for a few beers anyway. We both know I'm not into any of the guys here."

The beer is well within my bloodstream now, and I'm having a hard time keeping a straight face as I wait for my brother to make a decision. I can't slip up now, not when he's so close to leaving me alone. If I crack one buzzed smile, it's all over.

"Promise me you'll leave after a couple of beers, Aspen. Don't do anything stupid, especially when I'm not here."

"Pinky promise," I smile, holding up my pinky finger.

He grips my finger in his, wrapping them together as he pulls me into a goodbye hug. You'd think he was planning on being away from me for a long time, but the reality is I'll see him tomorrow at the hockey fundraiser. "Pinky promise," he hesitantly repeats back to me.

My friends and I watch him walk away, finding his spot amongst the crowd, then we turn back toward the bar.

"Finally!" Ashley gasps, slamming her hand down on the bar. "I thought he'd never leave!"

"He's just being protective," I laugh.

Brynne silently gestures to the bartender for another round, mouthing "thank you" when he nods, acknowledging her request. "Once Ace leaves, we're heading straight for that dance floor."

There's a small area off to the side of the bar where people are dancing, and I suspect as the night goes on and the alcohol continues to flow, more and more people will join in.

"I don't think I can wait that long," Ashley says, her voice coming out distracted and in a different place.

I turn to look at her, and that's when I realize she's locked eyes with a player across the bar. He's gesturing for her to come over, and she doesn't hesitate when I say, "Go, but be safe."

"Okay, Ace," she teases, giving me a look.

"I'm serious." I return the look, glancing back and forth between her and the guy across the bar. "He has on an NYU Makos hat. You know how gross they can be."

"I'll be careful," she rolls her eyes, then rises from the bar stool.

Ashley's hips sway in a hypnotic motion as she stalks toward him, her green eyes set on her prize. She's locked in on him, and I already know I'll be seeing him in the morning. Several of the men in the bar are staring at her as she crosses the room, and I can't really blame them.

She's absolutely gorgeous. She always has been. There's a natural beauty to her, enhanced further by eyelash extensions, lightly microbladed eyebrows, and a small amount of lip filler. Her hair is naturally wavy and full because of her Colombian roots. It's rare that she doesn't get the guy she wants. Who *wouldn't* want her?

Shortly after Brynne and I watch Ashley disappear into the crowd, we see Ace leave the bar. He's one of the first to leave, which is somewhat surprising, but he's always been even more focused on school than I have.

He's dead set on having a high-ranking corporate job in the city, but my dad thinks he can make it big in the NHL.

The watch on my wrist lights up with a text.

ACE

Don't stay out too late. Text me when you get home. They boys know to stay away from you.

I shake my head, still annoyed with how overbearing Ace has been tonight.

I quickly text him back for reassurance.

ME

I'll leave after this drink. No need to worry. Focus on your homework, not me.

He immediately responds.

ACE

Text me when you're home.

I sigh, rotating my watch away from my sight. The beer has settled into both me and Brynne, and I notice her eyeing the dance floor.

"Let's go," I say as I nod toward the growing group of people dancing.

"Really?" she asks. "You'll dance with me?"

The liquid courage is snaking its way through my

body, and I'm overly excited as I jump off of the bar stool. Grabbing her hand, I lead her into the middle of the dance floor. It's late, and the lights have been turned lower as the mood of the bar changes into something a bit darker, more thrilling. Brynne and I begin dancing, playfully grinding up against each other as the music feeds our souls, freeing us from reality.

Brynne's long brown hair cascades down her back, swaying in time with her hips as she dances, catching the eye of a large man wearing a Makos t-shirt. He steps closer to her from behind and grabs hold of her hips as she moves. She backs into him when she feels his touch, allowing her body to melt into his.

I'm left dancing by myself, but I don't mind with the strong buzz I'm riding. My eyes wander the room, finding Ashley in a corner making out with the guy she left us for earlier. She looks content and safe, so I continue dancing to the beat.

A man I don't recognize approaches me, and he begins dancing with me. He's wearing a ball cap with a hockey team logo on it, but I don't recognize it and I'm hesitant to dance with him. Everything in me is telling me to stay away. Hockey players are bad news and they're all in this bar for one thing: a slice of puck bunny.

If Ace were here, he'd be having a stroke right about now. Something stirs inside me, a little bit of rebellion perhaps, and I go against my gut feeling.

I begin dancing with him, keeping a little bit of distance between us as we move to the music. He's respectful at first, but it soon becomes apparent that he's had more beer than I have, and he gets a little grabby. I remove his hands from my ass, but continue dancing, trying not to ruin the mood or the vibe.

I look at Brynne, and she's completely lost in the music with the Makos player. They're bumping and grinding as though their lives depend on it, and there's sweat rolling down both of their faces now. She isn't even looking at me, so she doesn't notice when his hands begin roaming my body once more.

His hand slides up my torso, then suddenly cups my boob, squeezing tightly. I yelp, trying to jump away from him, but he holds onto me.

I turn to face him, and my voice does not waver when I say, "Let go of me."

The man doesn't acknowledge my words. He's too drunk to even comprehend that I'm speaking right now. He's sloppy and intoxicated. It's appalling, so I try to pull away again.

His grip does not budge as his hands continue groping my body.

I push against his chest, trying to get him off of me. "Let go of me!"

A large hand is suddenly on the man's chest, right in

front of my face, and I hear a male voice. "She told you to let go."

This catches the male's attention, and he's slow as he looks toward the man standing beside me. "What are you going to do about it?" The words are a slur as the alcohol takes hold of him even more.

The stranger removes his hand from the player's chest. His voice is cold as he says, "I'm going to take you out back, and I'm going to slit your throat. I'll watch you bleed out on the cold pavement while I sip on a bottle of top-shelf whiskey, and then I'll pour it over your dying body and set fire to it. You'll burn in *my* version of Hell long before you get to yours."

The music thrums through my ears, pounding against my eardrums, but I can hear him loud and clear. My blood runs cold when I realize he isn't making jokes, and he's really about to set this guy on fire. I close my eyes briefly, praying this drunk idiot has enough common sense to let go of me.

Releasing me, the drunk man glares at this stranger before staggering off into the crowd in search of a more willing piece of ass.

"Are you okay?" the stranger asks, pulling me out of the trance I put myself in.

"Y-yes," I stutter as I try to form words.

I glance around, looking for my friends, but they're

both nowhere to be seen. It's apparent they've both left the bar with the players they found. I'm here alone.

Looking back at the man, I find him still staring at me. He's a lot taller than I am, with dark brown hair and eyes that match, but I see specks of gold throughout his irises. He's gorgeous, but I need to get out of here. Tonight has been too much and I'm regretting coming out.

"Your friends left," he confirms. "I can call you a cab if you'd like."

Shaking my head, I decline. "It's okay. I need some fresh air and I don't live far from here, so I think I'll walk."

There's seriousness on his face as he watches me. "I can't let you walk alone. Let me walk with you."

I just met this man, and he's trying to walk me home in the middle of the night. There's still a little bit of a buzz circulating through my head, and I watch him for a moment, assessing the situation I'm in. He's wearing a black hoodie and jeans. He doesn't have a hockey logo anywhere on his body, so he seems like a safer choice than any of the other men in this bar. It's pitch black outside and I really don't want to walk home by myself, but I also don't want to spend money on a cab.

"You'll walk me home, then you'll leave? I'm not inviting you in," I say, letting him know where we stand.

A sparkle appears in his dark eyes, and a smile spreads across his face. "Just a walk."

"Okay," I nod. "Let's go."

"Lead the way." He gestures toward the door, then guides me there with a hand on the small of my back, maneuvering us through the crowd with ease. It almost seems as though people are parting for us, moving out of our way as we pass.

The breeze is cold as we step outside, blasting into my lungs as I gasp for a larger breath of air. I hadn't realized how shallow I was breathing until we stepped out into the open, away from the chaos inside the bar. He allows me to breathe for a moment, staying silent until I begin walking toward my apartment.

I still feel decently buzzed, and it encourages me to be more talkative than normal. He asks me questions about myself as we walk, and I'm more than happy to answer. What puzzles me, however, is when I ask him a question, he seems to brush it off and move on to the next subject.

"Why vet school?" he asks when we're over halfway home.

The wind passes through the fabric of my shirt, making me shiver and causing goosebumps to appear along my arms. My nipples harden, and I suddenly regret wearing such a thin bralette. I cross my arms over my chest, hiding the obvious peaks. "I've always loved animals. They're so much more forgiving and loyal than any human I've ever met. Plus, I've had an interest in medicine since I was in middle school, but I don't like people enough to be a doctor. Why help the cruel when I can heal the innocent?"

His hands are in his pockets as he walks beside me, and I can see him mulling over my response. "I'm not sure I've ever thought of it in that way."

"Most people don't," I admit. "The majority of the human population puts their lives above all other life."

He's silent as we approach my place. I'm not sure whether or not he liked my answer, but I suppose it doesn't matter, considering I'll likely never see this man again.

"Thank you," I say as we reach the walkway leading up to my house.

"It's been my pleasure," he smiles. "I'll watch to make sure you get in safely."

I fumble for my house key, pulling it from my tight jeans.

"Have a good night," I wave as I leave his side, heading for the front door. "Thank you, again."

"It was my pleasure," he smirks. Stepping through the door, I turn to watch him for a moment. He's standing tall, seemingly unphased by the chilly night. The body under his hoodie is athletic and built. I have zero doubt he could have taken that drunk idiot out back, but after talking with him for a while, I don't know if he's dark enough to slit a man's throat and set his body on fire. A shiver runs down my spine, and I shake away the feeling.

"Goodnight," I grin, closing the door quietly.

Locking the door, I slip out of my shoes before running toward the couch. There's a window behind the couch, but the blinds are closed, so I gently lift one of the panels to get a view of the man outside. He looks hesitant as he begins walking away, and he looks back at the house a few times. He can't see me, but it *feels* like he can. His dark eyes penetrate my soul through the glass, and my breath catches in the back of my throat.

Who is he?

A small bit of disappointment washes over me when I realize I'll likely never see him again. I don't know anything about him. He was dedicated to staying mysterious and uncooperative in answering any of my questions about him.

I sigh as I slide off the couch, rising to my feet. After checking both of my roommates' bedrooms and finding them empty, I send a text to our group chat.

ME

Made it home.

I copy and paste the same text to my brother, then strip out of my tight clothes and into an oversized t-shirt. My bed is warm and inviting as I climb into the white silk sheets.

My head is spinning from both the alcohol and the mysterious stranger I just walked home with. He was quiet, but he seemed to genuinely listen to what I was saying. I smile as I nestle down into the sheets, feeling giddy.

Visions of him play through my mind for several minutes before I force myself to take a melatonin gummy. I work early in the morning and can't be up all night thinking about someone I'll never see again. Within ten minutes, the gummy kicks in and I fall into a deep sleep.

Chapter Five

DUKE

The steaming water cascades down my body as I stand beneath the showerhead.

Fuck, I'm exhausted.

After last night, I barely slept, and that never happens. Girls don't get in my head. Not the way Aspen Anderson did. But of course, life would fuck me and make the hottest chick I've ever seen my rival's little sister. It's just my luck.

Of course, she'd be off-limits.

I run my hands through my thick hair to rinse the suds. I need to get a grip on myself. The way my blood boiled when that dude put his hands on her was out of line, and it can't happen again. Especially around the guys. One day, I'm going to end up following through with one of my threats and then I'll be fucked. But last night, I had to help her. I had no other choice since her friends and Ace fucking bailed on her. I couldn't just let that guy grope her. Not when every part of me wanted to be the one touching her.

Turning off the shower, I step out and grab the towel from the hook on the wall. I wrap it around my waist as I make my way toward the vanity. Wiping my hand through the dense condensation on the mirror, I quickly inspect myself.

Fuck, practice is going to be rough today.

I brush my teeth before heading out to the kitchen, where I have no doubt Jace Stanley is already waiting. That guy is the definition of a morning person. Some days, I regret letting him rent out my spare room. His morning smoothies and complete disregard for the fact that others might actually enjoy sleeping past 6 a.m. are a pain in the ass.

Rounding the corner, I find Stanley at the island in nothing but a pair of boxers decorated with pictures of tiny little slices of pizza scattered all over. His daily smoothie is in front of him, and his phone in his hand as he swipes up and down. Typical.

"Do you ever sleep in?" I ask sarcastically as I grab a coffee mug from the cupboard and head to the coffee pot.

"Who would have the coffee ready for you when you get up, sweetheart, if not for me and my early mornings?"

he asks jokingly. Cocking my brow, I look at him over my shoulder, and he winks.

"It's too early for your shit, save it for after practice." Grabbing the pot of coffee, I fill my mug and place it back on the heater. With the first sip, I suddenly find myself thankful that Stanley is up before me.

He's right. I can't remember the last time I had to brew coffee myself. The door to Stanley's room creaks open and a small girl slides out, clearly making her best attempt at the walk of shame as she makes her way toward Stanley at the island. That's when I realize it's Aspen's friend. The one who disappeared last night, leaving Aspen alone. She presses a kiss to his cheek and heads out.

My eyes snap to Stanley's to find him sporting a huge cocky grin. This fucking guy brings home a new girl every night. I have to admit I'm a little impressed. Turning around, I cross the small space and lean against the island on the opposite side of him. I eye him as I lift the steaming mug of black coffee to my lips again.

"What?" he shrugs. "It's the mustache man, I swear. They go nuts for it."

Unable to control myself, I burst out laughing. "There is no way in hell these chicks are letting you hit it because of your pathetic lip lettuce!" I add, placing my mug down on the island in front of me.

"Oh, please!" he snickers, running his thumb and

finger across the shape of his tiny mustache. The guys and I love busting his balls about it. He's been trying to grow that shit out since the day I met him three years ago and it hasn't changed. "Trust me, man, they love it. I'd tell you to grow one, but well, we both know you couldn't grow one as nice as mine anyway," he laughs.

"Fuck you, maybe I prefer my smooth baby face," I reply, whipping a small dish towel from the counter at him. He laughs, using his hand to block it, sending it to the floor. "Get the fuck in the shower, you idiot. We have practice."

Rising from his chair, he grabs the towel from the floor at his feet and whips it back at me. I duck to avoid it, sending it into the sink behind me. With his phone in his hand, he clicks the side button to check the time.

"Ah, fuck, you're right. Coach is gonna kick our asses if we're late. No doubt he already knows about us all being at Johnny's last night."

"Oh, I'm sure. There's no hiding shit from him, which means he's going to be extra tough on us today."

"'Cause he's not tough on us any other day?" Stanley laughs as he makes his way toward the bathroom. I lift the mug to my lips, tossing back the last of my coffee. The heat burns like hell but I know I need the caffeine if I'm going to get through this practice and keep my mind off Aspen.

COACH'S WHISTLE echoes around the empty arena. "Again!" he shouts.

The guys groan. I don't blame them. Coach is always hard on us, but today he's being a flat-out dick.

I stop in front of him, sending shavings of ice his way. I slide my glove off and spit my mouth guard into my hand. "Why? We all know the damn drill. We've done it so many times it's literally drilled into our heads at this point!" I snap. "We're all tired. Is running the drill again really worth risking an injury?"

Coach locks his eyes on mine, and by the look in his eyes, I know he's pissed. "Everyone but Stanley and Lexington hit the damn showers." From where he stands in the goalie net, Stanley and I exchange a look.

"Really? Come on, coach."

"Lexington, how many times are we going to have to discuss you staying out all night to drink?" he snaps, pointing his finger at me.

Stanley overhears and skates to us.

"Ah come on coach, it ain't his fault. He didn't even want-" Stone chimes in, his mouth guard sitting half out of his mouth.

"Stanley, no one asked you!" Coach snaps, cutting him off mid-sentence. He spits on the ice. "The season opener is in less than a week, and if the captain isn't taking training seriously, why should the rest of the team?"

"The Knights pulled up to Johnny's, Coach. Even you know Makos had to make an appearance," Stanley expresses.

Coach sighs, his head falling back to rest on his shoulders as he closes his eyes. "Was that little shit Anderson with them?"

"Fucking right he was. Cockly little fuck thinks he's brave showing up at Johnny's," I add, seeing an opening to get coach off our back.

"Nothing happened?"

Stanley and I both shake our heads. Any other night and it would be a different story. But I wasn't risking shit happening with Aspen there.

"All good though, we'll get him on the ice, yah? Alright, one more time, then hit the showers and get your shit together for the Little Leagues banquet. Keep your team in check tonight, Captain. I don't want to see anyone stepping out of line."

Fuck, how did I forget about that? The Little Leagues banquet is an annual event that the Makos attend along with every other team in the league. It's a fundraising event for the Little Leagues hockey teams in the lower Manhattan area and also a night to celebrate the upcoming season.

A whole night of fake people parading around,

spending money on shit that none of them actually give a fuck about, but it allows them to show off just how deep their pockets are.

"And next time, Lexington, have my daughter home by a decent hour. None of this 3 a.m. bullshit."

Olivia's late arrival has nothing to do with me, but I'll take the blame.

Coach heads off the ice towards the locker room. The high-pitched sound of his whistle echoes around the arena again. "Let's go, fuckers. The drill isn't going to run itself!"

Skating in a circle, Stanley pops his mouth guard back in and glides his hand back into the oversized goalie glove before banging his stick on the ice.

It was hard enough seeing Ace's stupid face in *my* spot last night. It took everything in me not to lose my cool and throw him out on the street. Now I have to spend the night with not only him but every other team in the league.

Perfect.

Sticking my mouth guard in my mouth, I pass the puck back and forth to myself as I skate down the ice. I deek around invisible players, side to side across the ice as I push the puck along the way. Stanley readies himself in the net with my approach, and I pull my arm back, setting up to take my shot. But I fake it, sending Stanley to the left side in an attempt to block it, leaving the right side wide open. I swing my stick back again, sending the puck flying right into the net.

He tosses his stick and gloves to the ice.

"Bullshit. You sneaky fuck," he laughs, spitting his mouth guard into his hand.

"Aw, come on. You should've seen that one coming," I reply, picking up his gloves.

Stanley skates in a circle around the back of the net as he slides his helmet off his head. Setting it down on the top of the net, he grabs his water bottle and squirts it in his mouth.

"You bringing Liv tonight?"

Like I have a choice.

Clearing my throat, I reply, "Uh, yeah. I have to pick her up on the way." He tosses the bottle back to the net and picks up his stick as he skates over to me to grab his gloves. "What about you? Swimming solo tonight like usual?"

"Yeah, but I invited Ashley to go out after."

"Who the fuck is Ashley?"

"The chick from last night," he mutters shyly. Stanley has never been one to see a girl more than once.

"Damn, she was that good, huh?" I joke, elbowing him as we make our way toward the locker room.

"Bro. Easily the best fuck of my life. No jokes," he adds with an excited tone. "The way she-"

"You can stop right there. I don't need to hear about your sexcapades," I cut him off mid-sentence.

He laughs, "She said Aspen will be at the banquet with Ace tonight too, eh. So you better keep your eyes to yourself unless you want to piss off Liv with dear old daddy around."

"I don't give a shit about Aspen," I mutter, doing my best to lie.

"Yeah, okay. And I don't jerk off in the shower after every game." I freeze, suddenly confused as to what the fuck he's talking about and why his jerking off has anything to do with Aspen.

"Okay, okay. Forget that. But the point is, Aspen is off-limits and you know it, Cap. No eye-fucking the enemy, especially tonight. I can't handle anymore of Coach's extra drills just because you've pissed him off."

"Yeah yeah, whatever," I add, shoving him into the wall as we make our way off the ice and down the narrow passage to the locker room.

Tonight is going to fucking suck, but at least I have an excuse to see her again.

Aspen.

Chapter Six

ASPEN

"What do you mean you don't know his name?"

"I... I didn't ask," I admit to Clayton, my closest coworker at the clinic. He's a vet tech in the same vet med program as me.

"You watched a devastatingly hot man threaten to kill a drunk, then you let him walk you home in the middle of the night, and you don't even know his name?" Clayton's voice is full of both disappointment and surprise. Not because he thinks I should be ashamed, but because he wants more tea than what I'm able to provide.

"Correct," I exhale as I offer him an embarrassed smile. "He seemed more interested in asking *me* questions than answering my own, and I was too buzzed to care. It's a lesson learned and I'll do better next time."

I've been thinking about the mystery man nonstop. He's flooded every corner of my mind since I woke up this morning. I'm pretty sure I even dreamt of him, but the remnants of alcohol in my body clouded my memory. I know it was mostly the alcohol encouraging me to ramble on and on, but he was *so* easy to talk to. I've never opened up to anyone as much as I did to him, and I basically spilled my entire life story to him last night.

"Damn right, you'll do better next time. How can you come in here talking about a mystery man, yet know nothing about him? You're depriving me of the hot gossip!"

"I know, I'm sorry! I talked his ear off," I groan. "How embarrassing is that?"

Clayton eyes me for a minute, then reluctantly says, "What if he was quiet because you were talking too much? Maybe he's one of those 'walk in silence' types."

My eyes widen with horror. "You don't think so?" I bite the inside of my cheek, contemplating his perspective. "He kept asking me questions, though. Or... What if he was being sarcastic and I didn't catch on? He probably thinks I'm an idiot!"

Mortified by the thought, I rub my temples, feeling a slight hangover from last night. Work came way too early this morning. Clayton and I had to be here at 6 a.m. to prep three dogs for surgery when the vets were scheduled to arrive an hour later. We spent several hours assisting the vets in surgery, then tending to the dogs and monitoring their vitals until they were ready to be picked up by their owners.

"I just think it's comical that you let him walk you all the way home and didn't even ask his name. We can't even look him up on social media."

"Next time," I promise as the bell to the front door chimes, signaling a client has entered the lobby. We've been waiting for the last dog to be picked up. "I'll take Rozzy out to her owner, then I'm off for the day. My dad is making me attend the Little League hockey fundraiser tonight. It's a big banquet full of rich-ass donors and brain-dead hockey players."

"I'll be here, wishing I was in a room full of horny jocks," Clayton sighs. He won't be off work until the night shift comes in at 6 p.m. We normally split shifts, but with all the surgery preps we needed to do this morning, he needed to be here early.

"I know you will," I laugh as I attach a leash to Rozzy, an eight-year-old beagle. "I'll see you later."

I walk with Rozzy to the front of the clinic and find her owner smiling and making conversation with our receptionist at the front desk.

"Here she is," I say as we round the corner, coming into full view. Rozzy sees Mr. Smith immediately, and she tugs at the leash as she tries to get to him. Little whimpers leave her while her tail wags a million miles an hour. "You need to take it easy, Rozzy," I say aloud, not because Rozzy needs to hear it, but because I want to politely remind her owner that she needs to stay calm and not jump around too much. For as old as she is, she still has a decent amount of energy.

Mr. Smith gets the aftercare speech from me, then I head home to get ready for the fundraiser. The drive is less than ten minutes from the clinic to my house, but it feels like forever. I'm beyond exhausted and ready for bed, but the night is still young when there's such a big banquet to attend. Dad would never allow me to skip it. For as long as I can remember, we've been going to this event. Hundreds of people show up for it every year. It funds all the Little League programs across the United States and Canada.

As soon as I get home I jump in the shower, washing away the grime of a long day at work. I squirt a handful of face wash into my palm and lather it between my fingers. It bubbles up and I rub it over my face in slow, massaging circles. A small moan slips through my lips at how good it feels, and I tilt my head back, allowing the hot water to rain down on my scalp. It's scalding, but that's perfect. The burn feels so good as it takes away the ache of the day.

I finish up in the shower, extending my five-minute makeup routine to fifteen minutes, and slip into my gown. It's deep navy blue, covered in sparkles, and there's a deep slit in it from the floor to my upper thigh. It's tight fitting, showing off all of my curves. Two little straps keep it up, ensuring my cleavage stays put. Ace probably won't love how revealing it is, but I feel *good* in it. I feel like me, and I feel absolutely stunning.

My phone buzzes, lighting up with a text from Ace.

ACE

I'm here.

Stepping into silver strappy heels, I do a once-over of myself in the mirror before leaving my room. Even I have to admit, I look hot as fuck.

Chapter Seven

DUKE

"Keys, sir?" the valet asks as I step out of my car. He's an older man, mid to late forties with thinning salt and pepper hair that he's combed back on the top of his head.

"Thanks," I reply, handing him my keys and a hundred-dollar bill. "Take care of her for me, eh?"

"Of course, Mister Lexington," he says as he climbs inside.

The engine roars to life as the valet starts it up and pulls away to park it in the lot. I make my way up the stairs toward the entrance of the venue. Scanning the crowd of people, I find Liv mid-way up the steps. She's chatting with a younger couple I don't recognize.

These types of events usually bring out the same people, so finding people I don't recognize is uncommon.

I still can't understand how I managed to attend this event all these years and somehow never noticed Aspen. Not that it matters now. I've definitely noticed her and tonight there's only one face I am interested in seeing.

Hers.

I haven't stopped thinking about her since the moment I saw her. I've gotten off to the thought of her three times already today, and it's still not enough.

Off-limits or not, I have to have her.

Noticing my approach, Liv giggles, "Ah, finally, babe. I was wondering what was taking you so long." She's pissed.

"Traffic, babe," I add.

Nodding my head, I exchange introductions with the couple that kept her entertained while she waited for me. I have no doubt that despite the cold tonight, she spent the entire time waiting outside for me. She'd never enter an event of this magnitude without me to parade her around and show her off. Image is every-thing to Liv, and tonight I don't even need to see the price tag of the godawful dress she's wearing to know it probably cost enough to feed an entire third-world country.

Tight fitting to her frame, the thin metallic gold piece of fabric barely covers her tits and shows way too much leg. Paired with the tallest heels she could find. As long as it's a brand name and gets her remembered, Liv will wear it. Unfortunately, there's no way anyone's forgetting this one for a while.

"Should we head inside then? I'm sure Daddy is wondering where we are by now," Liv asks, turning her brown eyes to mine.

"Yeah, let's do that. It's freezing out here anyways." I force a laugh that earns me an annoyed side eye as I lead her up the last couple of steps.

When we get inside, we stop by the coat check before making our way into the large main room of the venue. It's packed. There are at least fifty tables with ten or so people seated around each one. A live band plays soft music, and the dim blue lighting gives the room a calm yet expensive aura. The moment we're inside my eyes scan the room for Aspen. Liv's grip around my arm tightens as she leads me towards where our table is.

I spot Aspen a few tables away from us. Her dad and Ace are sitting with her, along with some of the Knights starting lineup.

She looks fucking gorgeous wearing a deep blue gown that looks like it was fucking made for her. Who am I kidding, even sitting down I can tell how well it hugs her perfect little body.

It was made for her.

"Hi, Daddy. This must be us, yep, here's your spot." Liv's voice hits my ears. Pulling my eyes from Aspen, I find Liv pressing a kiss to her father's cheek and I grab the back of her chair to pull it out for her. Once she's seated, I sit down next to her. Coach is on the other side of her and offers me a curt nod. "Sorry we're late. Poor Duke was stuck in traffic."

"You're not late," Coach replies to her as he checks his watch. "It's still early, give the boy a break, Olivia."

"I was just saying, Daddy..." she pouts.

Turning my eyes back to where Aspen's table is, I find myself utterly speechless at just how fucking beautiful she looks. She looks happy, inviting. She's chatting with the guy seated next to her, and by the patch on his suit, I can tell he's one of her brother's teammates. He's flirting with her. I can't help but want to break every bone in his body.

He'll get his.

When we meet on the ice, he's mine.

Mrs. Denninger, widow to Marcus Denninger, a former NHL player who still holds many records, heads out onto the stage in a ruby red dress. She waves her hand and the band pauses. Taking the mic in her hand, she turns her sights on the crowd of people.

"Welcome, ladies and gentlemen, to the New York Little Leagues fundraiser." The event starts, perfect timing. With everyone's eyes on the stage, the guy trying to hit on Aspen stops his attempts and turns his focus to the lady on stage. Liv pulls on my arm. Her way of telling me to pay attention.

I lift my eyes back to Mrs. Denninger on stage. She goes on to explain the fundraiser and where exactly the money raised tonight will go. Behind her, a PowerPoint slide spins with pictures of kids in the league and their smiling faces while they're on the ice. Carefully, I risk a look at Aspen to find her completely focused on the children in the slideshow. Her lips pull into a small smile as she places her hand over her heart and laughs as a picture of a kid pops up on the screen.

Just a little guy with a huge jersey hanging off his tiny body as he makes goofy faces at the camera. Adorable.

"Now you will see members of our team coming to your tables carrying a clipboard. They will be taking the donor's information over the next few minutes so if you wish to put a smile on a child's face, now is the time."

I flag down the first guy with a clipboard I see, and he rushes over. With my fingers, I direct him closer to my face so I can whisper in his ear from my seat. He does so and fills out the paper on his clipboard in the process.

"Thank you, sir. That's very generous of you."

"Of course," I reply. "Happy to help."

"Aw how sweet of you, babe. Don't you think, Daddy?" Liv purrs, running her hand through my hair. I hate when she does this and she knows it. She also knows another girl is getting my attention and since she clearly can't say anything about it at the moment, this is my payback.

"Yes, dear. Very generous of you, Lexington," Coach replies, offering me a nod.

He's impressed. Nothing says *"I can take care of your daughter"* more to the Upper East Side like blowing a few hundred grand at a fundraiser where anyone who matters can see it. Although it isn't all about money with Coach, it *is* to Olivia, and the only way to make her happy is to have pockets deeper than the Mariana Trench. I'll never understand how people can make money and status the center of their world. Don't get me wrong; I may have been born with money, but I don't give a fuck about it. It's never brought me a moment of genuine happiness or peace. If anything, it's created more problems, more expectations that I don't give a shit upholding.

I lean back in my chair, risking another glance towards Aspen's table.

Fuck.

From this angle and the way her dress hugs her frame, she looks like a goddess. My cock hardens in my slacks under the table at the sight of her alone. The thought of how good that body would feel beneath me crosses my mind.

Tapping the mic, Mrs. Denninger gains the attention of the crowd once more.

"The donations are in, and as a thank you, per tradition, we would like to announce the top donors of the night. First up, our third largest donation comes from

Mr. and Mrs. Johnston with a total of fifty thousand dollars," she announces, and the room breaks out in a round of applause. Mr. and Mrs. Johnston are well known on the Upper East Side. They own a few chain restaurants, but nothing super big or fancy. They came into their money seventeen years ago when Mr. Johnston won the local lottery.

New money.

That's what my parents call them.

"Next, our second largest donation comes from Madame Deloiox, with a total of one hundred and ten thousand dollars."

The crowd applauds again.

Madame Deloiox is also well known to anyone in New York who has money. She owns and manages the biggest escort service in the country. Shit, half the bachelors here tonight have one of her girls draped over their arm.

"Lastly, our largest and most *generous* donation tonight comes from none other than our very own New York University Makos captain, Mr. Duke Lexington, with a total of three hundred thousand dollars," she adds excitedly before bringing her hands together.

People turn their focus on me from their chairs, nodding and applauding. I thank them, returning their nods as I wave my hand above my head and scan my eyes across the crowd. But the moment they land on Aspen's eyes, the entire room seems to disappear and I find myself sinking in their ocean depths.

Liv's hand on my thigh tightens, pulling me back.

"Really? Three hundred thousand dollars? Where did you even get that kind of money?" she seethes through clenched teeth against the shell of my ear.

"Who said I don't have money?" I laugh as I grab the glass of water from the table. People have turned their attention back to the woman on stage as she continues her speech.

"I just didn't know *you* did," she spits, leaning back in her chair. Around us, servers make their way into the room carrying trays of steaming food that they deliver one by one to each table.

"Why would you?" I reply with a hushed tone just as the server places my tray in front of me.

THE NIGHT IS COMING to an end. The rest of the event went smoothly, surprisingly. However, I'm not entirely sure what I missed seeing as I spent my night fixated on Aspen and the guys from her brother's team who are seated around her.

"This place is dying down, can we go now?" Liv asks as she sulks in her chair. She's been itching to leave since Coach did shortly after dinner.

"I already told you to go. I don't know why you're waiting on me."

"Because Duke, we should be seen leaving together, don't you think?"

"Not really. Who the fuck cares? You came here without me, don't you think they expect you to leave without me, too? And honestly who is even paying that much attention to what people do?"

"People notice things," she snaps. "You think I haven't noticed you watching her? Your new little obsession?"

My eyes slowly move to Aspen, angered by the fact that Liv has the balls to mention her. "Shut up, Liv," I spit, bringing the glass to my lips.

"Whatever, I'm out of here. It's your ass on the line if people think something is up between us, remember? Not mine." She storms out, her heels clicking along the tile floor as she makes her exit.

She's not wrong. It is *my* ass on the line, and as annoying as Liv is, I should cut her some slack for keeping up this act with me. Only a few people remain at the fundraiser, one of them being the only reason I haven't left yet. Aspen. Ace and his team left hours ago, but she stayed back to help clean up, and even though it's late and I have early practice, I haven't been able to tear my eyes off her.

So, here I sit, like a shark. Hunting my prey.

Chapter Eight

ASPEN

The fundraiser went smoother than any other year I've attended. Unfathomable amounts of money were donated this evening, and I'm still in shock. There was enough money donated to fund every single Little League in both the United States and Canada for the next year. Any kid wanting to participate in hockey will have the opportunity and money won't be an issue.

My heart warms at the thought of less fortunate children having the opportunity to play one of the most expensive sports free of cost. I can't even imagine the weight it'll take off the parent's shoulders when they find out they won't be paying a single penny for this season.

The success of the event put me in an unusually good mood, so I volunteered to clean up the banquet room at the end of the night. Ace was supposed to be my ride home, but I wanted to stay and he was dead set on getting home to study for one of his big tests. When he tried to convince me to leave with him, I told him I'd find a ride using one of my ride-share apps.

As I clear the last of the plates from the round tables I pull my phone out of a pocket sewn into my dress, then put in a request for a ride, but it's immediately clear no one is out driving tonight. Taking a glance outside, I realize just how hard it's beginning to snow. The white powder is heavy as it clings to the ground, coating everything in a thick blanket. It's coming down so hard I can't see more than a few feet out the window, and it's well into the darkness of night.

Sighing, I slide my phone back into my pocket and cross the room to set a stack of dishes next to the woman elbow-deep in hot soapy water.

"That's the last of it," I smile as I wipe my hands on a wet dish towel. "Is there anything else I can help with before I head out of here?"

Amy, the woman in charge of the volunteers looks up at me from across the room. "If you could take the trash out to the parking lot on your way out, I would appreciate it."

"Of course," I nod. "Thanks for letting me stick around and help out."

She laughs before saying, "I should be the one

thanking you. Several of our volunteers called out at the last minute and I thought we'd be here all night. You worked efficiently enough to make up for at least three of my regular helpers."

"It's my pleasure," I laugh gently, my cheeks blushing from her praise. "Have a good night."

She waves me off as I pull the last trash bag from the pile that had been sitting beside the door. The bag is heavy as I grip it, pulling it off the ground. I'm pretty sure people threw away full drinks and didn't bother emptying them out beforehand. The snow blasts my face as I open the double doors and step outside. A shiver runs down my spine, raising the hair on the back of my neck, but I brush it off as being nothing more than a chill after doing a quick scan of the parking lot. I can't see much. There are only three cars left.

Amy's, her assistant's, and a car I don't recognize.

I wonder who else would be here this late?

Shaking my head, I assume someone had too much to drink and left their car. Snowflakes land on my long lashes as I stalk across the parking lot with the heavy bag. The trash barely clears the side of the dumpster as I heave it over, but it makes it.

My phone vibrates and I pull it from my pocket once more, checking to see if anyone has accepted my ride request, but there's radio silence on the app. No one is out driving in this storm. They'd have to be out of their minds to risk driving strangers around in exchange for mediocre tips. My phone dies just as I'm about to switch over to a different ride-share app.

Fuck.

Wrapping my arms around myself, I begin walking home. I can't ask Amy or her assistant to drive me. They live on the opposite side of town and I overheard them both talking about what little gas they have left in their cars and how terrified they are to drive in the snow. They don't get paid for several more days and they can't afford to put more gas in their cars until then.

It's only ten blocks away. I can do it in ten minutes, give or take a few depending on how slippery it gets. When I chose these heels I wasn't imagining my night would end like *this.*

Streetlights guide me as much as they can, but it isn't much. The snow is coming down even harder than when I first stepped outside. It's cold, but the snow is more wet than anything. It's drenching my gown, making each stride harder than the last. Stray strands of hair slap against my face as they blow in the wind.

I don't make it more than a hundred yards before I hear a car approaching me from behind. I can barely see it, but I recognize it as the car from the parking lot. The darkly tinted window slides down and a familiar face comes into focus.

It's the guy from the bar. I noticed him at the

banquet tonight, but there was a girl hanging all over him. She rubbed her hands along his forearm as he placed bids on numerous items donated to the auction. My jaw dropped every time he raised his card, alerting the auctioneer of his bid. He spent hundreds of thousands of dollars tonight.

He's smiling at me as he says, "Can I give you a ride?"

I laugh as I hold my arms against my cold, wet body. "You already walked me home, and now you want to drive me in the worst storm of the year?"

His smile fades slightly. "If I wouldn't let you walk home alone on a beautiful night, what makes you think I'd allow you to risk your life in a snowstorm? It's getting worse and we both know you shouldn't be walking, especially by yourself."

My walking slows, and I turn to face him. I'd be stupid to not take him up on his offer. "Can that car make it in this snow?"

He doesn't hesitate. "Yes, now please get in the car. I don't want to drag you in here, but I will if I have to."

My eyes widen at the thought of him physically forcing me into his car, but I'm almost excited by it. "What's your name?" I ask.

"Duke," he beams. "Duke Lexington." There's a playful charm to his voice, like he's proud of the name he bears.

"Aspen," I say in return. I take a step forward, then

whisper, "Fuck it," as I get into his fancy matte black Lexus 300. The rich leather aroma hits my nose immediately as I duck inside, seeking safety from the storm. It's immaculate. Not a speck of dust anywhere, and here I am, dripping water and snow all over the black interior.

I sigh, closing my eyes as I lean my head into the headrest and allow myself to breathe. The leather mixes with his sandalwood and citrus scent. The concoction is intoxicating as I inhale it, euphoric almost.

"All set?" he asks, an eyebrow raised as he watches me through whiskey-brown eyes.

"Yes," I nod. "My phone died. I don't normally walk home alone like this. You've caught me twice now, so I'm sure it looks like I'm a loner, but I've just been put in unfortunate situations this week."

"Is it unfortunate I found you tonight?" He almost sounds hurt by my choice of words, so I correct myself.

"No. That's not what I meant at all. I just meant I've had a weird week, that's all. It's nothing you've done."

He's quiet for a moment, then says, "Good. Charge your phone." He points toward a wireless charging station installed in the center console.

"Thank you," I smile as I set my phone down in the center of the charger, making sure it's charging before moving my hand away. I feel tension in the air as my fingertips linger between us, but then visions of his brunette girlfriend jog my memory. "Do you remember where I live?"

He glances over at me and I watch the street lights shine across his face as the car moves down the road. "Of course."

Curiosity gets the best of me, and I can't help myself. "You didn't mention you had a girlfriend the other night. She's very pretty."

Clearing his throat, he's serious as he speaks. "She isn't my girlfriend."

I let out a laugh. "She's not? That's not what it looked like when you had her hanging off your arm while you funded half the Little League by yourself."

"You noticed?" his lips curve into a smirk. "I was almost getting the impression you didn't recognize me."

"Of course, I recognized you," I let out a soft giggle. "I mean, I thought it was you. I didn't even know your name and we've only met once." Shaking my head, I realize he's trying to change the subject. "What's *her* name?"

He's quiet again. "Olivia." His knuckles shift from a tan shade to white as he grips the steering wheel. "She's not my girlfriend."

"Who is she then? The two of you looked pretty cozy at the fundraiser."

I shouldn't care. I shouldn't even be asking because it's really none of my business, but I find myself feeling jealous. I've been thinking about him nonstop ever since he left my house. It hurts to find out he avoided one major detail: *her*.

My phone buzzes as it comes to life in the center console, catching both of our attention. I grab it, then read the texts popping up on the screen.

ASHLEY

Power is out. No heat and no hot water. Don't come home if you don't have to.

I groan, letting my hand fall into my lap with my phone.

"What's wrong?" he asks, his voice curious.

"My roommate texted me. The power is out at my place." Rubbing my hands through my wet and tangled hair, I feel disappointed knowing I won't get a hot shower or central heat to warm me back up when I get home.

Duke hits his brakes, then turns the steering wheel, making the car drift. We're facing the opposite direction before I can even say anything. "I'm taking you to my place. You're too cold to go somewhere without heat."

"I'll be fine," I argue, glancing back in the direction of my house. "I don't think Olivia would like another woman staying at your place." Her name rolls off my tongue with bitterness.

"Fuck Olivia," Duke spits. "You're coming home with me."

"No, I'm not," I laugh. "I am not about to start a feud between you and some girl I've never met. She made it clear to everyone in the room that you are hers, and no one else's. I'm not getting involved in that."

A low, frustrated growl escapes from his throat. "It's all fake. We aren't dating and it's all for show. Her dad is the coach for the team I play on, and I keep my captain's seat because he thinks we're together. She has a high profile appearance across social media and it makes both of us look good to be together. We benefit from the world thinking we're a couple, but the truth is I can't stand the thought of actually being with her. Have you looked at her? Fake tits, fake eyelashes, fake everything. I want something *real,* and she isn't it." The word vomit flows from his mouth as he falls over his words. "You are coming back with me and we're going to get you warmed up. You aren't getting involved in anything by spending *one* night at my place. I'd like to do this for you."

My lips part as my jaw drops. He's admitting a secret far darker than any I've ever kept, and he's trusting me with this information. Is it all for show? For social media likes, a career push, and clout?

We're both silent as we sit, processing the information he dumped on me. I almost feel like an idiot for not picking up on it, but how could I? I barely know the guy. He walked me home *once*.

"What happens if someone sees us going to your place together and reports back to Olivia? Or posts it online? What if word spreads that you're cheating on the coach's daughter with the rival's little sister? Then what?"

"It won't happen," he shakes his head. "My penthouse is discreet and no one will see us. I'll make sure of it."

He's driving faster than I'd dare to drive in the storm and he's getting farther and farther away from my little house.

It's like he can hear my thoughts, and he knows I'm actually contemplating going back with him. "I have a fireplace," he says as he reaches toward my side of the car, gripping my ice-cold fingers in his rough, but warm hand. Instinctually, I go to pull away, but he's holding me firmly. "Please," he pleads.

"I don't *need* you to do anything for me," I correct him, but I don't pull away.

His voice is soft. "I *know* you don't, but I want to. It's just one night, and nothing needs to happen."

"Okay," I give in. "One night, and you'll take me home in the morning when the power comes back on."

He's smiling from ear to ear. "Deal."

Chapter Nine

DUKE

Pulling into my parking spot in the underground parking of my penthouse, my head fills with concern. I just told Aspen about my fake relationship with Liv. Why? I have no fucking idea. I haven't even told the guys it's fake and I know I can trust them with anything. But Aspen? Somehow even barely knowing her, she's got this pull on me that has me wanting to tell her anything and everything, so long as it keeps her here with me.

It's dangerous.

She is dangerous.

As we make our way inside, I watch her eyes light up with wonder at the sheer magnitude of the building. The penthouse suite was a gift from my parents for my twentieth birthday, not that it was something I wanted. They more or less thought it necessary. They couldn't have their circles on the Upper East Side talking about their son and how he's living in the dorms with the rest of the college kids. That honestly would've been perfectly fine for me.

"This place is insane," Aspen whispers, running her hand along the smooth concrete wall. I laugh, pressing the button next to the elevator before sliding my hands in my pockets. Her eyes roam the long and elegant hallways, taking in every inch of it all. "I can't even imagine what it must cost to live here. It's nice." Her eyes find their way to mine, which have been glued to her since we walked in. "What?" she asks.

"Nothing," I smirk. "You're right, it's a nice building, but the most beautiful part about it right now, is you."

"Does that work with all the girls?" she laughs cheeki-ly. The elevator dings and the doors slide open. I follow her inside.

"Don't know. Fake girlfriend and all, I haven't really had a chance to test it out," I explain, pressing the pent-house button.

"Right," she adds. We lean against opposite walls, facing each other as the doors close. Her ocean eyes lock with mine as she tucks a loose curl of her hair behind her ear.

God, she is fucking perfect.

My cock hardens as I watch her pull her pouty bottom

lip into her mouth with her teeth teasingly. She knows exactly what she's doing, and she loves it. We hold each other's stare as the elevator makes its way up to the twenty-ninth floor, where my penthouse sits at the top of the building. The silent seconds pass slowly, each one spent making it harder not to cross the small space and pin her against the wall. Especially in that goddamn dress.

Bringing her here wasn't the best idea I've ever had, even though inside I'm fucking pumped she's at my place. Keeping my hands off of her is going to be harder than I expected. Off-limits or not, tonight, Aspen Anderson is the enemy's net and there's not a goalie in sight to stop me from scoring. The bell dings again, signaling we've reached the top floor, and the doors open up to reveal the main entrance to my penthouse.

"The penthouse? Really?" she smiles. Finally breaking our gaze, she pushes herself off the elevator wall and heads inside. My eyes follow her, watching the way her tight little ass sways in her fitted gown as she walks ahead of me.

Control yourself.

I need to get a grip. She's off-limits.

She's a Knight.

"Why do you sound so shocked?"

The entrance opens up to a large open living space with a wall of crystal clear windows that overlook downtown New York. The decor is all matching. Different shades of gray and blue with the odd fake plant my mom's interior designer shoved on a shelf or table to give the place a little touch of nature.

"I don't know," she replies as she spins in a circle, her eyes taking everything in from the smooth tile floors to the crystal chandelier that hangs from the sixteen-foot ceiling. "Just doesn't feel like *you*."

"And you would know what *feels* like me? You've known me for what, two days?" I laugh.

"You know what I mean. Although I will say, I can believe you and Oliva aren't actually dating after seeing this place."

"Oh, so you didn't believe me before?"

"I mean, anyone can lie and say their girlfriend isn't their girlfriend. Guys do it all the time, but, having seen this place, there's no way in hell you guys are *actually* dating. This place has 'bachelor pad' written all over it."

"I don't know if I should be offended or glad," I laugh.

Fuck, she's got a little feisty side to her.

My cock hardens again, and I immediately know I need to focus my attention on something else. "Let me get you some clothes to change into," I say, kicking off my shoes as I slide out of my coat and hang it over the back of the gray sectional in the center of the living room.

"Oh, right. Yeah, that would be great. Thanks,"

Aspen replies as she makes her way to the windows. "This view is fucking incredible."

Looking up, I find her slowly sliding out of her jacket. In the dim lighting of the penthouse, her silhouette next to the snowy cityscape is easily the most beautiful thing I think I've ever witnessed.

"Yeah, million-dollar view," I reply with a hushed tone as I make my way down the hallway.

Reaching my closet, I open it, grab a pair of my boxers and a plain tee, and place them on the counter in the bathroom across the hall for her. Opening the drawer in the oversized vanity, I pull out a brand-new toothbrush and a small tube of toothpaste and place them on top. Stanley has a stockpile of them for the revolving-door of chicks he brings home for the night.

I make my way back out to the main living space and find her still taking in the sights of the city from way up here. The penthouse is silent. The wind outside from the winter storm whistles, blowing glittering snowflakes against the large windows. "I left you a change of clothes in the bathroom."

She jumps at the sound of my voice. "Right, thank you," she replies.

I watch as she kicks off her heels, and bunches up the fabric of her gown. Her eyes find their way back to mine, and she smiles as she heads to the bathroom. The door clicks behind her.

Making my way to the large modern kitchen, I open one of the top cupboards and pull out a bottle of my favorite whiskey. "What's your drink of choice?" I shout, my voice echoing around the open room.

"What are my options?" Aspen calls back to me.

"Well, I wasn't really expecting guests, so we're sort of limited," I laugh. "Whiskey, rum and I think I have some wine in the fridge."

"White or red?"

Pulling open the oversized stainless steel fridge door, I grab the bottle of wine that one of Stanley's guests left here.

"Red."

"Perfect," she replies. I jump, having expected to hear her voice from the bathroom but instead, her soft voice comes from behind me. Spinning around with the wine in hand, I find Aspen on the other side of the island, wearing my Makos practice jersey.

Well, fuck me.

Her long ashy hair is hanging in loose beach waves down her back, and the makeup she wore tonight has been washed away, leaving her completely natural and utterly beautiful. The jersey hangs off her shoulders and is so oversized I can't even see the boxers I know I gave her, but hope she's not wearing.

"Hope you don't mind. It was hanging on the back of your door and well, it looked warmer than the shirt," she admits with a cheeky smirk as she brings herself to stand next to me. "Where do you keep the glasses?"

I find myself speechless.

The sight of her in my jersey has me unable to form words. My eyes scan her up and down, taking in the sight of her in Makos colors.

I'm fucked.

As if I wasn't already struggling to keep my hands off her tonight. Blue is her color, but not just any blue. Makos blue.

Still unable to find the words for everything my head is thinking, I point to the cupboard behind her, directing her to the glasses as I place the bottle of wine on the island. She spins on her heel, giving me her back as she crosses the small space to the cupboard.

LEXINGTON.

The sight of my name on her back makes my heart stop.

It makes me feel things I know I shouldn't.

That's my fucking name and my number.

And fuck if it doesn't suit her.

"So, you're a whiskey guy, huh?" she asks, her voice soft and alluring as she stands on her toes to reach the glasses.

"Yeah, I guess you could say that," I finally manage to utter. She places the glasses on the marble counter of the island and takes the bottle of wine, popping the cork out before she pours herself a glass. I follow her lead, filling my glass with a few inches of amber whiskey. Our eyes lock as we both lift the drinks to our lips. The liquor burns as it glides down my throat, but I welcome the pain. "We should sit," I add, directing her toward the large sectional.

"Yes, please. My feet are killing me after wearing those god-awful shoes all night."

"I will never understand why you women put your-selves through it. I mean sure, they make your ass look great, but I don't think you need to suffer for that."

"Oh? So you think my ass looked great tonight?" she smirks cockily as she sits down next to the large window. She pulls her legs up into her chest and covers them with my jersey for warmth as she eyes me flirtatiously.

Fuck. My lips pull into a grin as I take a seat next to her.

"I mean, I may have checked you out a few times," I admit, shaking my head at her as I bring the glass to my lips again.

"And what did you think?" she asks curiously.

"Honestly, I think you're easily the most gorgeous girl I've ever had the pleasure of laying eyes on. Even without putting yourself through hell in those," I reply, nodding my head toward where she left her shoes.

She smiles, flashing me a glance at her pearly white teeth before tossing back the remaining wine in her glass and placing it on the table. Her ocean blue eyes sparkle in the dim lighting as she slowly moves towards me, and slides herself onto me. Taking my glass, she places it on the table next to hers.

"What are you doing?" I ask.

Holding my confused stare, her eyes fill with hunger. "No one has to know but us. I want this, Duke. And I know you do too," she whispers against my ear, raising goosebumps along my skin.

My hands instinctively find their way to her hips and slide under the thick fabric of my jersey to find that she never put the boxers on but left on her little lace thong. A growl vibrates through my chest, and I grab the back of her head, pulling her lips to mine. The kiss is hungry and filled with a need unlike anything I've ever felt. Aspen feels like everything I've craved for so long but never knew I was missing.

Her hips grind against my hardening cock as she teases my tongue with hers. I let her take full control.

"Just this once," she utters in soft breaths against the shell of my ear.

She slowly slides her hands to my jeans and unbuttons my belt. Her hand slips inside, freeing my hard cock from both my jeans and my boxer briefs. She strokes it slowly, wrapping her soft hand firmly around its thickened girth. My head falls back as moans slip from my lips. She peppers soft kisses down my neck and shoulders as she sits straddled over me.

"Pull them to the side," she mutters before her lips slam over mine again.

Fuck, this is really happening.

I do as she says, reaching between her legs to pull the thin fabric of her lace underwear to the side, holding them in place as she lines herself up.

Breaking our kiss, I whisper, "Are you sure you want to do this?"

She doesn't answer. Instead, she crashes down on my cock, taking its full length in one movement.

"Jesus," I groan, my grip tightening on her hips as I hold her in place.

It takes all my willpower not to bust from how tight her pussy is gripping me. My chest rises and falls fast as she wraps her arms around my neck, pulling my face to her chest. My jersey hangs off her shoulder, revealing some of her flushed flesh to me. Just when I think I have control over myself, she begins to rock her hips, slowly.

Fuck.

Her arms loosen their hold, and her head falls back as she finds her groove and begins to ride me. Looking up at her, I sink my teeth into the exposed flesh of her collar.

"Oh fuck, yes," she cries out before picking up the pace.

The sex is carnal. Full of passion and hunger. The

way she moves on me like she's needed this as badly as I have.

"Aspen," I whisper, knowing if she doesn't slow down, I'm not going to last much longer.

"Yes? God, Duke, you feel so fucking good," she whimpers before her lips once again find mine. Frantically, she grinds, keeping her eyes locked with mine while her wet pussy glides up and down my shaft with the guidance of my hold on her hips. Lifting my hand from her hip, I lower it to her round ass, smacking it. The sound echoes around the empty penthouse. "Fuck. Yes. Again, please."

"Fuck, Aspen. You're gonna make me-" I moan into her mouth as I bring my hand down on her ass again, harder this time. My hand finds its way back to her hip, gripping her tightly and guiding her motions. Bringing my thumb to her mouth, I run it along her soft lip before pushing it into her mouth. Like the good girl she is, she wraps her lips around it and sucks on it. My cock twitches inside her as I pull my thumb from her mouth and lower it to her clit, moving it in circular motions as she rides me.

"Oh, yes," she moans. Her body convulses over me, her pussy clenching down around my cock as her orgasm hits her.

Unable to fight the urge anymore, I follow her lead, emptying myself inside her as she rides out her orgasm.

She collapses against my chest and my head falls back against the couch.

Did that *really* just happen?

Fuck. I just fucked the enemy.

"We're a sweaty mess," she laughs.

"That we are," I reply, wrapping my arms around her. "Shower?" I ask.

Slowly, she tilts her chin up, resting it on my chest as she lifts her eyes to mine. "That would be great," she says, slowly climbing off me. She adjusts herself while I tuck myself back into my boxers.

"So uh, we didn't use any protection and well, I-"

"I'm on the pill, don't worry about it," she laughs as she gets up from the couch and makes her way toward the bathroom.

My lips pull into a smile at the sheer sass this girl has. I fucking love it.

But if watching her walk away with my name on her back and a pussy full of my cum doesn't make me feel some type of way...

Just once is never going to be enough.

Not with Aspen fucking Anderson.

Chapter Ten

ASPEN

It's been a week since I've seen or heard from Duke. It's been one week since we fucked in his penthouse and had the most incredibly mind-blowing sex of my life.

We never exchanged contact information, so it's not like I can just text him or get ahold of him without looking him up on social media like a creeper. I don't want to come across as obsessive as I'm feeling. There's a hunger I've been feeling all week to get back to him, to let him back inside me and share the euphoric high of secretly fucking my brother's biggest rival.

Tonight, I'm going to the first game of the season. Ace isn't playing the Makos tonight, so I don't expect to see Duke at the game. He has no reason to attend a

Knights game, but a small part of me hopes he'll be there scouting out the competition.

Ashley and I walk into the cooled stadium together, beers in both hands. As soon as we turned twenty-one we started using my brother's hockey games as an excuse to drink and let loose. My dad expects me to attend every one of Ace's games, and I want to be the most supportive sister I can be, so I make sure I'm here, but I don't have to be sober the entire time.

We're meeting up with one of Ashley's new fuck buddies. I haven't met him yet, but she said he plays for the Makos. They've only been talking for a few days, but Ashley moves fast with these hockey players. They don't stick around for more than a couple of weeks anyway, so it works out well for her.

My jaw hits the floor as we turn down the row our seats are in.

"There they are!" Ashley squeals, quickening her pace as she makes her way down the row.

I struggle to form words. "You... You didn't mention your friend was bringing anyone else with him."

"I knew you wouldn't agree to it if I told you ahead of time, so surprise! This is Jace and his roommate, Duke." Ashley shrugs her shoulders, beaming as she sits beside her fuck buddy. She has no idea what she's done.

Duke mentioned he had a roommate, someone from

the team who needed a place to crash for a while, but I didn't know Ashley was banging him.

I frantically try to pull myself together as I sit in the *only* open seat.

Right between Ashley and *Duke,* who is sitting comfortably beside none other than Olivia.

Bile rises in the back of my throat. She has no idea what we've done. Ashley has no idea how awkward and incredibly fucked up this entire situation is.

Duke's warm scent fills my nose as I sit beside him. I don't know what to say or what to do.

Do I acknowledge him? Do I act like I know him? Or are we complete strangers?

I can feel his eyes on me as I look around the arena, trying to find my brother warming up on the ice. Anything to distract myself right now.

His gaze grazes across my bare skin as he watches me. I'm holding my breath, and I don't know when I'll breathe again.

Olivia rises from her seat. "We need to take some pictures together for a post I'm going to make later."

Duke is quiet as his eyes leave me and find her. He's visibly annoyed with her, but I don't know why. He's the one who put himself in this fake relationship with her. I get why it benefits both of them, but why do they have to lie to literally *everyone* around them?

He stands and then follows her to the end of the row

where the aisle opens up. There's fire in my eyes as I watch them. It's not audible to my ears, but it looks like Olivia asks someone to take a picture of them with her phone. Olivia wraps her arms around Duke's neck, pulling him into her. What pisses me off most is when Duke doesn't hesitate to slink his hands around her waist, pressing his hard body into hers. Just as they're about to kiss for the picture I stand up, no longer able to control my emotions.

I need to leave.

I need to get the fuck out of here. I can't watch them for another second, and I sure as shit can't sit here with them once they come back to their seats.

With Duke distracted by Olivia, I turn toward Ashley, trying to level out my voice as I say, "I'm not feeling well. I need to go home before I get sick."

"What's wrong?" Ashley sits up, giving me her full attention for the first time since we've arrived. "You seemed fine before we got here."

The lie comes easier than it should. "Yeah, it must have been something I ate earlier. I'm going to head home. Can you find a ride?"

"I'll take her back to my place," Jace smiles, wrapping his arm around Ashley's shoulders as he draws her into him.

Duke's place. The thought overwhelms me, and I feel an oncoming anxiety attack. I need to leave.

"I hope you feel better," Ashley smiles. "I'll text you tonight to check in and see how you're doing."

Faking a smile as ingenuine as Duke and Olivia's relationship, I wave goodbye to Ashley and Jace, and slip out before anyone else sees me. I walk as quickly as I can to the exit and take a sudden turn out the door and into an empty hallway where I can breathe for the first time since I sat down.

Covering my chest with my hand, I back myself against the wall and lean forward, trying to get some air. It's too much. I'm falling for him too quickly and I'm a fucking idiot for it. I knew what I was getting myself into when I fucked him a week ago. I *knew* she wouldn't be going anywhere and that our little secret would have to remain a secret.

I have to be his secret.

But I don't want to be anyone's secret. And who am I kidding? I'm keeping a secret of my own.

I've fallen head over heels for my big brother's rival. If my dad or Ace find out, they'll not only lock me up and keep me hidden for life, but they'll go after Duke. They'll be out for *blood*.

Tears well in my waterline and when I feel like I can't keep it inside anymore, that's when a door swings open. Fast footsteps make their way down the hall, getting louder with each stride. Raising my eyes, I find Duke heading straight for me.

Shaking my head, I put my hand up and say, "No," as I turn away from him, rushing toward the nearest exit. If I can just get to my car, maybe he'll leave me alone.

"Aspen, please," Duke shouts from behind me, but I keep going. I can hear him getting closer, and it pushes me to keep going.

"I don't have anything to say to you." Tears are nearly falling from my eyes now. "Go back in there, or they'll be suspicious of us both leaving."

"I'm not going back in there without you." Duke's voice is desperate.

"You can, and you *will*," I laugh as I push the exit doors open, stepping into daylight.

He follows me through the doors, across the parking lot, and to my little Buick. I pull out my key to unlock my car door, but he's around me before I can get in. His hands rest on either side of me as he leans against the car. I close my eyes, pushing away what my heart wants as his scent envelops me and the warmth of his body presses into mine.

"Please don't leave," he begs. "I know it's hard, but we can find a way to make it work."

"I already told you I don't want to get involved with you if you're with her, real or not. Everyone thinks you're together, and I refuse to be anyone's second. I refuse to be anything but someone's entire world. I deserve more than *this*," I say as I gesture between us.

The gold flecks within his eyes catch in the light, drawing me into his unfathomably handsome features for a few seconds before I force myself back into reality. It doesn't matter how hot he is, how much money he has, or what he says.

This won't work.

We have everything working against us even without Olivia in the picture. My family will never let this happen. We'll never know anything more than sneaking around.

"Just give me some time..." he trails off. "Wait until the end of the season and I'll come clean. I'll end things with Liv and we can be together."

Liv.

The nickname rings through my mind. Of course, he has a nickname for her. Jealousy takes over, and I feel my face flush with heat.

"This won't work," are my final words as I get into my car, slamming the door shut before he can get another word in. He looks broken as I back out of the parking space and speed off with tears in my eyes.

Chapter Eleven

DUKE

"Fuck," I moan as I pump myself. The heated water from the shower cascades down my body as I vigorously fuck my hand. My head is filled with thoughts of Aspen. Her blue eyes and how fucking sexy she looked riding me the other night while she wore my jersey. Fuck, she felt good.

Better than good.

I've craved her and dreamt of her ever since.

I fuck myself faster, harder as that night replays in my head. The sweet sounds she whispered in my ear as she found her release. She wanted me as badly as I wanted her, and even though she's mad at me right now, I know she still does. My balls tighten with impending release, and I tighten my grip, mimicking the way she clenched down on me. It's enough to bring me over the edge. I slam my palm against the tile wall to balance myself.

"Fuck yes, baby. That's it. Just like that."

Jets of white cum shoot out from my cock's tip as once again I find release to thoughts of the one girl I'm not supposed to want. The one girl I'm supposed to stay clear of but can't because from the moment I saw her I've been completely consumed. My body shudders with the last of my release, and I quickly wash off before turning off the tap. Opening the large glass paneled door, I grab the towel from the hook and wrap it around my waist.

Yesterday didn't end well with Aspen, and because of that I barely slept. Watching her drive off last night hurt. It hurt more than I expected it to. I fucking miss her. Today, she has no choice but to talk to me. I don't care what it takes but Aspen will be mine. She has to be.

Grabbing my phone from the vanity, I swipe it unlocked and open Facebook. Finding the search bar, I type in her name. I've never been big on social media. I'm perfectly fine going days without seeing what that weird kid from high school is eating for dinner, or the bathroom selfies from that one girl I banged in the club bathroom in junior year.

What I'm not fine with is not knowing how to get in contact with Aspen.

Her name is the first to pop up.

The small bubble next to her name is a picture of her as she holds a fuzzy cat up to her smiling face. Clicking her name, her profile pops up and I scroll down looking for a way to contact her. Where most people have a message option, hers is off.

Great.

Further down, I find something I can work with.

Apparently, she works at Beatties Animal Clinic. A quick Google search tells me they're open today, and it's not too far from the university. Closing my phone, I pull out some clothes and start getting dressed. I'm going to that damn clinic, even if I have to adopt a fucking animal to get in there.

I PULL up to the small clinic. It's in a quiet part of town, and by the looks of it, it does well for itself. Not that I'm surprised. I don't have any pets of my own, but I've heard they can rack up vet bills pretty quickly.

Inside, I find a line of chairs along a wall on the right. Some have people sitting in them, holding their cats or dogs, while most are empty.

It's not busy. Good.

To the left is a small room with shelves of food and toys people can buy for their pets after their appointments. For a building dedicated to animals, it doesn't smell bad. It smells clean, like a hospital. With a hint of lavender.

"Can I help you?" a woman asks, pulling my attention. Following the voice I find a large curved desk in the center of the room. She stands behind it with her auburn hair in a messy bun and her hand on her hip.

Slowly, I approach her. "Yeah, sorry. Um, I'm looking for Aspen?"

"Aspen? That's odd. She doesn't usually handle solo patients. Okay, what's your pet's name so I can bring up the file?" She takes a seat in her rolling desk chair and begins clicking away on her keyboard to log in to her desktop.

"No, I don't have a pet. I-I don't want to bother her while she's working, I just need to know if she's here today?" I reply, resting my arms on the counter of the desk.

She pauses, her eyes rising to meet mine.

"Right... Yes, Aspen is in the back, should I get her for-"

"No. No, that's fine, thank you. What time do you guys close?" I ask.

"We close at 4:30 p.m. today, sir," she replies. Her eyes fill with judgment. She's unsure of me and untrusting. Which is good. It means Aspen's co-workers care about her. It's just after four now, meaning they'll be closing soon.

"Perfect, thank you for your help," I say before heading back out of the small clinic and into the parking lot. Reaching my car, I grab my coat from the backseat and slide into it before taking a seat on the hood of my car. No way I'm allowing her to leave after her shift without at least talking to me.

AFTER WHAT FEELS like hours of sitting in the snow and cold, Aspen finally makes her way out of the clinic. I watch from the hood of my car as she bids her co-workers goodbye. The auburn-haired one from the desk eyes me, causing Aspen to turn her sights on me. She's wearing teal scrubs, similar to the Makos blue color of my jersey she wore when she rode me on my couch the other night. A night I refuse to forget.

Fuck.

Part of me hoped she'd be happy to see me. I mean, I looked up her work just to find her. That's kind of romantic, right? But by the look on her face as she trudges through the snow towards me, I can tell happiness is not what she's feeling. She's pissed.

My cock hardens in my sweats, and I'm forced to readjust myself.

"What the fuck are you doing here, Duke?" she spits as she approaches.

I smirk, finding her annoyance a turn-on. "Isn't it obvious? We have shit to talk about, and you don't make it easy," I smile, sliding off the hood of my car. Tucking my hands in my pockets to keep them warm, I bring myself to stand in front of her.

Her ashy blonde hair blows about in the wind, filling my nose with the citrus scent of her shampoo. Her cheeks and nose are rosy from the cold, making her eyes pop.

"Maybe because I don't want to talk to you. I mean, take a hint," she snaps. "I'm not into guys with girl-friends, even if they're *fake*."

"Just listen, okay? Aspen," I plead, kicking my boot into the snow. "I can't just end it with Olivia, not yet and not just like that. It's too complicated. But that doesn't change that *you* are the one I want to be with."

"That's a fuck boy quote if I ever heard one," she says flatly, holding my stare.

"I'm not a fuck boy and you know it. You know the deal with Olivia and I, and you know damn well I haven't wanted anyone, not the way I want you, Aspen."

"That doesn't change anything. You need to leave me alone," she shakes her head as she makes to leave.

"No," I snap, stepping in front of her to stop her from leaving. "This isn't how shit ends for us. I know we barely know each other, but I can't stop thinking about you. You're all I can focus on Aspen, and I want us to see where this can go. To give this, *us*, a real shot. But I can't. Not yet."

"What do you mean 'not yet'?" She raises her voice. People leaving the parking lot look at us in wonder.

I sigh, doing my best to calm my tone. "Just give me till the end of the season, that's all I'm asking. One season of keeping our secret."

She crosses her arms across her chest, "And then what?"

"At the end of the season, I will end it with Olivia, and we'll be together, publicly."

"No," she replies as she tries to step around me.

Shocked by her response, I step in front of her, cutting her off again. "No? What do you mean 'no'?"

"Listen, Duke. I like you, a lot. More than I thought I would, and I believe you'll do all the things you're telling me you will. Honestly, I do. But that doesn't change the fact that you're a Makos. Not only are you a hockey player, but you play for the rival team. My dad and Ace will never accept me being with you." I can tell by the way she breaks our gaze and lowers her eyes to the snowy ground that those words stung as she spoke them.

Sliding my hand from my pocket, I grip her chin, lifting it to force her beautiful eyes back to mine and smile. "They won't have a choice. Don't you see it, Aspen? I'm not taking no for an answer. I want you, and I know you fucking want me too. So they either accept it, or fuck them."

She doesn't respond right away, her eyes flickering back and forth with mine as the cold winter wind whips around us. By now the parking lot has cleared out, and the sky is growing dark.

"Just one season..." she stammers.

"Just one season, baby. One season of secrets and then the world will know who you belong to," I whisper, lowering myself to ghost my lips over hers.

"Okay."

"That's my girl," I smile against her lips, before kissing her. She kisses me back, her lips parting ever so slightly, allowing my tongue to meet hers. Wrapping my arms around her, I pull her into me, deepening the kiss as my mouth catches her soft moans.

"Can we go now?" she laughs. "I'm freezing,"

"Yeah, let's go. My place?" I ask, pressing a kiss to her forehead. "Stanley is out for the night. I'll order us some pizza and we can get you all warmed up."

"You had me at pizza," she winks, pulling herself from my hold. She makes her way to the passenger side of my car, smiling at me before she climbs inside.

My head falls back and my eyes find their way to the sky.

Thank fuck.

Things are far from perfect, but I got my girl, and that's all that fucking matters.

Chapter Twelve

ASPEN

I knew Duke wouldn't be able to resist this red lace bra and matching panties after practice, and that's why I'm leaning over the side of a bench in the Makos locker room, long after practice has ended. Duke's eyes lit the moment he saw my hot little number underneath my scrubs, and I couldn't stop myself from letting him take me right here and now.

The locker room was empty when we came in, the air thick with the scent of sweat and ice. The dripping of the showers made goosebumps pimple along my skin, knowing we could get caught at any moment if someone were to come back.

His fingers are laced through my hair, pulling tightly as he slams into me from behind.

"God, Aspen, you're so fucking sexy bent over for me like this," he groans, his voice thick with need.

I smile, feeling a surge of energy from his words. "Show me how much you want me," I whisper, pushing back against him as he quickens his pace.

"You don't need to tell me twice," he says as he turns me around, forcing me to walk backward until my shoulders slam into the cold metal lockers.

"Ah," I half moan, half wince as he presses all of his weight into me.

He raises his hand to my jawline, cupping my face and my neck as he draws me in, devouring my mouth with his. Our tongues collide as though it's the last time, and the reality is, I think that's why we fuck like wild animals. We crave each other's touch, yet we scarf it down so rabidly and quickly that it's over before we know it. Taking our time puts us at a higher risk of being caught, and we can't do that. Not with so much on the line. We're in too deep now and I don't know how we'll ever stop.

The end of the season can't come soon enough. My urge to murder Olivia every time I see her posting a photo of them online only increases each day. Over the past few weeks, I've gotten pretty damn good at avoiding seeing them in person, but there isn't a whole lot I can do online when everyone I follow shares and likes their shit. Part of me lusts for him even more because I know he's not fully mine. Sharing him with a fake girlfriend is even harder than I predicted it would be.

Reaching down, I run my hand over his bare cock, feeling his hot skin and pulsing veins. He lets out a groan, and his hands grip me tighter. His hand is wrapped so tightly around my neck that I can feel him cutting off my airway, but I fucking love it. My eyes widen at the sight of him so undone and on edge with me.

Duke presses into me harder, pinning me in place against the lockers as he kisses me fiercely. His hands roam across my body as he lifts me up, allowing me to wrap my legs around his waist. I gasp as I feel him poking against my entrance. The friction of him rubbing over me makes me moan, and I let my head fall back against the lockers as I wrap my arms around his neck for support.

Running his hands up my thighs, his fingers dance over my clit before pressing more firmly, rubbing in slow circular motions. He dips a finger inside me, wetting it before returning to my clit to swirl around it some more. It glides more easily with my arousal covering his fingertips, and I feel my climax building deep within my core. I try to grind against his hand as I seek more friction, but he's got me pressed up against the lockers so hard I can't move. I let out a frustrated moan as he slips his finger back inside me, withdrawing for a second before inserting a second, then a third. He's filling me with his fingers, drawing out every drop of pleasure my body can handle.

I glance up for the first time in a while to find his eyes, and he's staring into my soul. His plump bottom lip is sucked between his teeth as he watches me unravel through darkening eyes. The gold specks in his irises have morphed, puddling into streams of molten gold.

Dropping to his knees, he throws my legs over his shoulders, forcing me to straddle his face. His tongue flicks over my clit, making me jolt as the pleasure hits me. My back arches off the lockers as I moan, "Oh, Duke."

I can feel his smirk against my pussy as he moves lower, his tongue diving into my folds as he devours my flesh. I inhale sharply, biting my bottom lip as I tangle my fingers through his hair. I instinctually begin grinding against his face, rocking my hips against his mouth and riding the waves of pleasure crashing over me.

Just as I'm on the brink of exploding, he pulls away with a mischievous grin on his face.

"What are you doing?" I groan, my body aching for release.

"I'm only getting started," Duke replies, standing up and pulling me to my feet. He turns me around, bending me against the lockers as he positions himself behind me.

My heart is racing and it only pounds harder when I feel his hard cock pressing against me. I lean back, impatiently trying to push him inside of me. He lets out a soft chuckle when he realizes how needy I'm feeling. I *need* to feel him inside me, to be completely consumed by him.

He doesn't waste any time, thrusting into me in one powerful stroke. I cry out as the feeling of him filling me sends shivers down my spine. He's so *big,* so *hard,* and every thrust leaves me breathless and wanting more.

Duke pounds into me, his body slamming against mine with each thrust. I can feel my orgasm building as my walls tighten around him, my pussy begging for release.

"Fuck, Duke, don't stop," I moan, the pleasure becoming almost unbearable. I could scream right now, but I can't risk it, so instead I press my teeth into my own arm, biting down as he fucks me.

Reaching around and gripping my hip with one hand, Duke's other hand moves to my clit as he continues driving into me. The added pressure is enough to send me over the edge, making my body shudder and my legs weaken as an orgasm rips through me. His grip tightens on me as he feels me clenching around him, his own release following shortly after. He buries himself deep inside me as he comes, his body trembling with the same intensity as my own.

We stay like this for a moment, catching our breath and basking in the afterglow. Duke finally pulls out of me and helps me find my balance, kissing me softly before pulling me into his arms.

"That was amazing," I whisper, my head resting against his chest as our pounding hearts slow.

Duke chuckles, amusement and satisfaction in his eyes. "You always amaze me, Aspen."

I smile, looking up at him through thick lashes. "I wish we didn't have to sneak around like this. I hate it."

His face falls slightly. He knows I'm growing increasingly frustrated with our secrecy, but he can't risk anyone finding out and jeopardizing his career. And I can't risk my dad or Ace finding out about this.

"I know, baby," he says, brushing a strand of hair behind my ear. "We have to be careful a little while longer."

I let out a sigh, the frustration evident in my voice. "I just wish we could be together without all this hiding and sneaking around. I get it, but I hate that it's like this. It's not fair to either of us."

Pulling me closer, Duke wraps his arms around me. "I know, but for now let's focus on the time we have together and make the most of it."

I glance up at him, studying his face. I know he's doing the best he can, but I can't help but feel like I need more and that I'm deserving of more than this. I shouldn't be a secret left in the dark, and neither should he.

We stand here for a few minutes, lost in each other's arms before Duke finally breaks the silence. "I have something to show you," he says with a mischievous glint in his eyes. "I don't think anyone is coming back this late in the night."

He shines his watch at me, showing me the time. It's past midnight.

Raising an eyebrow at him, I'm intrigued by his sudden change in demeanor. "What is it?"

He smiles as he leads me to his locker, opening it and pulling out his duffle bag. It takes him a few seconds to rifle through it, but he eventually holds up his skates with a devilish grin on his face.

"We're going to play a little game," he says, his tone playful yet sexy.

My eyes widen with both excitement and surprise. I don't know what he's up to yet, but I can already feel the ache burning between my thighs.

Grabbing my hand in his, he quickly leads me out of the locker room with the skates and his bag. The cold air of the arena hits me as we step through the doors completely naked. Suddenly I remember we're in a public building and we're supposed to be sneaking around.

"Are you sure this is a good idea?" I ask as I scan the empty arena.

"No one is coming back. If anything, the boys are all out drinking tonight."

He pulls me onto the ice, and all I have on is my shoes. The ice is slick as we walk, but he leads me across it with ease, keeping me upright and balanced. As we near one of the goals, Duke suddenly turns and pulls me into his arms, his lips crashing into mine. I moan into his mouth, my craving for him, coming back to life with each touch.

Pulling away, Duke eyes my naked body, surveying every bare inch of me. Finally, he says, "I want you to lie down on the ice."

"You want me to what?" I laugh as I choke out the words. "I'm naked!"

His face is serious, unwavering as I question his sanity. He circles me, then points to the ice. "I asked you to lay down, Aspen."

He's leading me on a wild goose chase and I still have no idea where he's going with this, but I decide to trust him. I lower myself to the ice, wincing as the frozen ground bites at my skin.

"On my back?" I ask.

"Yes," he nods, watching me so intently I feel like I might melt under his molten gaze. "Then spread your legs for me."

Doing as he says, I lean back, letting the backside of my body rest against the ice, then I widen my legs, giving him a full view of my pussy.

"That's my girl," he smirks as he takes one last look at me before diving back into his duffle bag.

I watch him quietly, taking in our surroundings. I've never experienced the arena this quiet before. It's silent other than our movements, and the air is just cold enough to take my breath away. This ice under my body isn't helping, and I can feel myself beginning to shiver.

Duke lowers himself between my thighs, tossing the bag a few feet away. In his hands are his skates and a roll of athletic tape. He pushes my legs further apart as he scoots closer to me.

"Give me your hands," he says, reaching for them before I have the opportunity to offer them to him.

The coolness of the ice is beginning to fade into a numbing sensation, burning as it frosts my skin. The hot and cold feeling has me flustered as he wraps the athletic tape around my wrists, securing them together before using his teeth to tear it off the roll. He's naked too, and I can't stop myself from watching his hard cock move with his body as his muscles flex.

His tone is still serious as he begins speaking, drawing my attention back to his face. "I'm going to do some things that are going to be uncomfortable, and they'll hurt a little, but I need you to trust that my end goal is to bring you more pleasure than you ever thought possible. This is for *both* of us, Aspen. Can you do that?"

My mind is racing and the idea of being caught is still in the back of my mind, but I silently nod.

"I need to hear you say it."

A lump in the back of my throat makes me choke on my words, but I force them out. "Y-yes. I can trust you."

Duke's eyes darken further as my words wash over his ears. He brings his lips down to my level, stopping beside my ear. "I'm going to bring you so much pleasure you'll never want to leave me."

Little does he know, he's already done that. I'm completely and utterly lost to this man. He's taken over every corner of my soul and I belong to him far more than I'm willing to admit.

My lips part to speak, but he covers them with his own, warming them as he deepens our kiss. The feeling of cold metal presses against my leg, and then my body jerks as I feel a sharp pain. I gasp, opening my mouth to cry out, but Duke doesn't let me. He cups my mouth with his hand, shaking his head as if to tell me to be quiet.

I watch him glance down to where the pain is emanating from on my leg. He smiles, then rubs his fingertips over the stinging spot. It hurts more as he presses against my flesh, gliding his fingers around and spreading warmth, which I realize is my blood as he brings his fingers to his mouth, eyes locked on mine. He dips a blood-coated finger into his mouth, gently swirling his tongue around it. His mouth closes around his fingers, and then he sucks them clean, not leaving a single drop of my blood.

"Mmm," he groans as he tastes me, his eyes rolling back as his lids flutter. His cock hardens even more against my body as he leans over me, pressing it against my entrance. He's teasing me.

I'm shocked as I watch him devour the crimson liquid, but I'm so intrigued, and even more turned on by what I'm watching.

There's a smudge of blood on Duke's bottom lip, making him look primal. Feral almost.

Duke sits back on his heels, still between my spread legs. He picks up one of his hockey skates, which has a thin layer of my blood dripping from it. Bringing it to his fingertips, he runs the sharp blade against his flesh, opening it as the metal glides. The red liquid shines in the low arena lighting.

Pressing his lips to my ear once more, his voice is dripping with desire as the blood drips from his fingers onto my cold, bare stomach. "I want you to ride me while I fuck your mouth with my fingers, Aspen. Show me how much you want me."

I can't resist him. My body instantly responds to his command. Hands tied tightly, I grip him with my thighs, then force our bodies to switch positions. We roll, and I end up on top, straddling him. Using what little range of motion I have in my hands, I grip his cock, then guide it to my aching pussy. I glide it along my folds, wetting it before seating myself on him, allowing his cock to sink deep inside me.

The ice is slippery, making it hard to move gracefully,

but I eventually find the right tempo. My body moves up and down, occasionally grinding into him for even more pleasure. He fills me so fully that I don't think it would be possible to fit anything else inside of me. Using one hand to rub a thumb over my clit, Duke pushes my body into oblivion. I have an orgasm rising so quickly that I feel like I'm falling apart, becoming numb to the euphoric sensation.

As my orgasm begins, Duke presses his bloody fingers to my lips. "Open."

Lost to the pleasure, I open my mouth, granting him entrance to my mouth. He slips two fingers inside, rolling them over my tongue and coating it in his blood. The taste is metallic as it spreads across my taste buds. I thought I'd be repulsed, but it only drives me deeper into my orgasm. Duke's fingers press further into my mouth, hitting the back of my throat and triggering my gag reflex. His grip on my mouth is so firm I can't actually gag, and my body responds to his movements. I'm trapped under his will, coming undone as I ride his cock and let him fuck my mouth. All I can do is moan around his fingers, quietly crying out as I shatter around him.

Removing his fingers from my mouth, Duke grips my hips, forcefully thrusting himself into me and pushing me down harder. "Let go, Aspen. That's it."

Without his fingers in my mouth, I forget where we are and I cry out as my orgasm rips through me. My body shakes with pleasure as Duke follows me over the edge, his body tensing as he comes with me.

I collapse against his chest, both of us breathless and spent. I lay on top of him, feeling the perfect combination of the coolness of the ice and the warmth of his body.

"That was perfect," I say, my voice barely above a whisper as I look up, finding his eyes.

They've returned to a more tired, but casual Duke state. The animal inside him seems to be tamed.

He smiles, brushing a strand of hair out of my face. "Only with you."

We lay together on the ice for a few minutes, catching our breath before finally making our way back to the locker room for our clothes.

I can't help but feel a sense of sadness as we dress and prepare to go our separate ways.

I hate the thought of leaving him, even if it's just for a little while.

<h1 style="text-align:center">Chapter Thirteen</h1>

DUKE

The elevator door dings as it reaches my penthouse floor and slides open. I drop my hockey bag on the floor in the entrance as I head inside. Every inch of my body fucking hurts, yet I can't wipe the smug grin off my face. Fucking Aspen. Never did I think a girl could make me feel so many things. After Olivia, I didn't expect to ever trust a girl again, let alone care for one, but with Aspen, things are so different. *She* is so different. She's real, and she drives me fucking wild.

As I make my way into the main living space, the familiar sound of Call Of Duty hits my ears, followed by Stanley shouting at the TV. Guy is never willing to admit he's straight dog shit at the game. Any time he dies, he blames whatever poor soul he's teamed up with, and it always results in a huge screaming match. I'll admit, most nights it's fucking annoying, but tonight, nothing can kill my mood.

"Fuck off! What the fuck are you doing, you idiot? Shoot him!" Stanley shouts into his headset as I round the corner. "Oh fuck off, how do you miss every shot, bro!"

"Sounds like you're having a great night," I smirk.

Sitting down on the couch next to him, I pull my phone from my pocket and kick off my shoes. The table is littered with empties and munchies, a sure sign he's been at this for at least a few hours and he's probably been getting his ass handed to him the entire time.

On the ice, Stanley is a fucking machine. Guy's got more talent than half the team put together and has reflexes that would blow your mind. But when it comes to first person shooter games, well, let's just say I've seen middle school kids with better KDR than him.

"Oh yeah, sure. It would be a lot better if this fucking twat could actually shoot the enemies instead of leaving me to carry," he spits. I can hear the sound of his team screaming back at him through the speakers in his headset, but typical Stanley ignores them and carries on. "What took you so long to get home? Practice was hours ago, man."

"Aww you keeping tabs on me, mommy?" I laugh, whipping one of the small square couch pillows at him.

"Bitch, don't do that shit," he shouts with a high

pitched tone as he blocks the pillow with his arm and tries to stay alive in his game.

I laugh, picking the pillow up from the floor. "I had some shit to handle, alright?"

"Yeah, okay. Since when are you so secretive, Cap?" he asks, keeping his eyes focused on the TV screen.

"Since I needed to be. Don't worry about it," I reply as I lean back into the oversized couch. I watch as Stanley dies in the game and the audible screams from his teammate once again blast through the speakers of his headset. He pulls the headset down around his neck and looks over at me.

"You're good though, yeah?"

"Yeah man, shit's great," I nod.

"Alright, cool. I'm going to order Chinese. I'm fucking starving," he says, placing the controller on the table. He heads towards the kitchen in search of the menus.

"Eh, get those spring rolls too," I shout over my shoulder.

"You got it, Cap,"

My phone lights up in my lap, and I see notifications from Carter Bishop, a rookie forward from our team. Not a bad kid, but he's ambitious and that can be dangerous. I flick open the message and notice he sent me a video. Stanley is on the phone in the background, ordering

Chinese food from the place down the street as I click play on the video on my phone.

It loads for a second and then plays. At first, it's just dark, until Aspen comes into view. But it's not just her. It's a video of her and me in the locker room after practice today.

This mother fucker.

Rage builds inside me instantly. I watch, unable to tear my eyes from my phone as the video plays out. She's pressed against the lockers... there's the pink flush that coats her skin, and her gorgeous face as she moans with pleasure while I fuck her. The fact that this piece of shit got to see her like that infuriates me, but what's worse is he recorded it.

The video ends, and it returns to the message window.

> **Bishop**
>
> Fucking the enemy are we, Cap? The team deserves better. I want your patch, Duke, or the world, including that little rich bitch you call your girlfriend, will see this video. You have a week.

What in the actual fuck?

I whip my phone across the room. Bringing my clenched fist to my mouth, I sink my teeth into it to keep from losing my shit. My chest rises and falls rapidly as I contemplate my options. I can't risk this video coming out. I'm not willing to let it affect Aspen or the relationship she has with her dad and Ace. I might not like the guy, but I care about Aspen, and I know if they find out about us from this video, it will blow her entire world up.

"The fuck is that about?" Stanley says with raised eyebrows, making his way back into the living room. He places two beers on the table before making his way over to where my phone landed. He picks it up and hands it to me. "Luckily you didn't break your screen again. The fuck is going on?"

"Nothing, I'll handle it," I snap, taking my phone from him. I tuck it in the large front pocket of my hoodie.

Stanley plops back down on the couch and grabs his headset before pausing and handing the controller to me. "When I'm pissed, I kill people. In Call Of Duty, of course. Where, you know, it's legal. It helps."

"I'll pass, thanks."

"Suit yourself," he sighs, sliding his headset back up over his ears.

Giving Carter my patch means I will no doubt lose a lot of the scout support and probably end my hockey career for the NHL before it even begins. It means my parents will lose their shit, and if the coach finds out I'm banging someone other than his daughter, who's to say he'll let me stay on the team?

I'll lose everything.

But her.

She's enough, though. For the first time in my life, something, *someone* means more to me than hockey. More than my career in the NHL. If giving it all up is what needs to be done to protect her, then that's exactly what I'll do.

No regrets.

Chapter Fourteen

ASPEN

I texted Duke after I got home last night, but he hasn't texted me back yet, which isn't normal. For the past few weeks, we've been texting constantly when we aren't together, completely infatuated with each other's company and time. After what we did last night on the ice rink... I thought we connected more than ever, but now I'm having doubts. I don't understand how we can go from drinking each other's blood to radio silence.

I don't know. Maybe I'm overthinking it and something came up. He *does* have a life outside of me, after all, and sometimes I find myself forgetting. The days until the end of the season are ticking down, slowly diminishing. Time has been moving both in slow motion and incredibly fast since the beginning of the season. On one hand, I feel like I've known Duke forever and he's the easiest person to get along with, but on the other, each day hiding in secrecy has felt like an eternity. It's becoming harder and harder to keep this secret from the people I love.

I swore to Duke I wouldn't tell Ashley until the season is over, and I've kept my promise. She's my best friend, so she naturally suspects something is up, but she has respected my boundaries and accepted my answer when I told her I would let her know what is going on when the time is right.

Ace has been so caught up in schoolwork and hockey he hasn't had much time to check in on me. The Knights have done unusually well this season with Ace as the captain and my dad coaching the team, and they've worked their way into the finals.

My phone buzzes in the pocket of my scrubs, and I immediately feel for it. My heart stops beating and I stop breathing as I pull it from the fabric and read the notification on the screen.

I sigh and drop my head slightly as I read it.

ASHLEY

I'm staying at Jace's tonight. Don't stay up. I'll see you tomorrow.

I should be happy to get a text from my best friend. I mean, she's thinking about me enough to send me a text and let me know what she's doing. She didn't want me staying up late after work, waiting for her to get home. I type out a quick reply, then slide my phone back into my pocket.

I can't help but wonder if I did something wrong or said something I shouldn't have last night before we left the rink. Everything seemed fine, but sometimes Duke gets quiet, lost in thought.

Forcing myself to shrug off the feeling, I grab my car keys and head out the front door. I have a nine-hour shift at the clinic today and I can't let myself be distracted by the thought of Duke all day. I don't take up all of his time, so he shouldn't take up every thought in my mind.

Sliding into my Buick, I shut the door and insert the key into the ignition. The old engine comes to life as I turn the key. Before I back out, I find myself reaching for my phone again, checking to see if I missed a notification in the past thirty seconds.

Nothing.

My phone is as dry as the Sahara Desert.

Sighing, I throw the car in reverse and leave for work. I'm sure I'll hear from him by the end of the day. I'm overthinking it.

"Lexington, what are you doing here? Practice isn't for a few hours still," Coach explains as he greets me outside his office. Little does he know, I've been here for way longer. After Carter's text last night, there was no way I was getting any sleep. Not until this bullshit is dealt with and I know Aspen is safe. Coach unlocks his door and heads inside his small office.

"I needed to talk to you," I reply. Lifting myself from the cold concrete floor I've been sitting on for half of the night, I follow him inside and close the door behind me.

"Alright then, son. What is so important that you couldn't wait?" he asks, taking a seat in the small wooden chair behind his desk. He powers up his computer before turning his attention to me.

Fuck, here we go.

My heart is racing in my chest, a sure sign my nerves and anxiety are kicking in. "I want you to take my patch, and give it to Carter," I admit.

Coach furrows his brows with confusion. "Bishop?" he laughs. "And why do you think the rookie should have your patch? The patch the team voted for *you* to wear. Do you not think it's an honor to have such a symbol stitched into your jersey?"

"No, of course not. Fuck, I know what it represents, and of course I want it. But I can't keep it. Carter has to have it, okay? Just, give it to him." My palms begin to itch and I rub them along my thighs hoping the friction will ease the annoyance.

"Alright, enough. Tell me exactly what is going on here," he says, crossing his arms over his chest as he leans back in his chair.

Coach isn't stupid. He's known me long enough to know when something is up, and it's clear not only that this is out of character for me, but also that I'm stressing.

"Duke, what's going on?"

"I'm not dating Olivia. We've been broken up for almost a year," I admit. After keeping the secret for so long, I thought it would be harder to admit it, but it isn't. If anything, I already feel a bit relieved.

"Okay, well as much as that's a surprise to me, I must be missing something. What does that have to do with giving your patch to Bishop?" he asks as he tries to make sense of everything.

"I've been seeing someone, and well, when I was with her last night in the locker room, which yes, I know, is against the rules, Bishop saw us. He recorded us, and is blackmailing me for my patch in order to not have it go viral," I explain.

Coach eyes me sternly, making reading his reaction impossible. What feels like hours of silence pass before he suddenly bursts out laughing. "That's it?"

My eyes widen with shock. "Uh, well yeah."

"Listen, boy. I don't care that you and Olivia aren't together. I do, however, care that you lied to me about it. She's my daughter. I love her but she's a spoiled brat, thanks to her mother and honestly, I thought it was a miracle you lasted as long as you did putting up with her nagging." Coach pulls out a cigar from his pocket and places it between his lips as he sparks it up. "Secondly, you'll definitely be doing extra laps, not today though. I can tell by the look of you that you don't have them in you today. Also, you wouldn't be a hockey player if you didn't get a little bit of locker room action. As for your patch, no. It stays with you."

"Coach, you don't get it. I *have* to give it to Bishop. It's not just me on the line here."

"That's too bad. The rookie isn't cut out for the captain patch, you and I both know that. I don't know who this girl you're banging is, but it doesn't matter. Even if Bishop is stupid enough to blast the video, he's never getting that patch. The team voted for you, and I signed off on it. You're keeping it, kid."

What the fuck am I supposed to do now? How do I keep Aspen safe if I can't do what Bishop wants?

"What I can do for you, is make it clear to Bishop that you tried. I will let him know you came to me, and that I refused. Maybe then he'll at least lay off you and the girl," Coach adds before taking a long drag of his cigar.

"You shouldn't smoke, it's-"

"Finish that sentence, Lexington, and I'll reconsider my decision," he warns sarcastically. A smirk forms on my lips. It's not what Bishop wanted, but it may be enough to at least protect Aspen.

Hopefully.

"Go home, get some rest. You clearly need it. I'll handle Bishop."

"Now, how would it look if the captain skipped out on practice because of a little loss of sleep?" I laugh, pushing myself up from the chair across from him. "I'm good, Coach, honestly. I'll grab a coffee from the lounge and go stretch while I wait for the guys to get here."

"Before you go, I want you to know. Regardless of what happens between you and my daughter, you're like a son to me, Duke. I'm going to do what it takes to make sure you get to where you deserve. There are always going to be little shits like Bishop in your career path. The key is to not let them stop you." His voice is stern, and I know he's right.

Bishop's little power move may have allowed him to get me right where he wanted me, but it was only because of Aspen. I'd give up anything to make sure none of my bullshit touched her.

"Thanks, Coach," I say before heading out into the hall. I close the small office door behind me and make my way down the narrow hall towards our locker room. While I probably should've taken Coach's advice and skipped out on practice, there's no way I'm missing it. Not after Bishop had the balls to pull this shit. No, I'm going to look that fucker in the face today when Coach tells him. I'm going to sit there and watch him as he accepts defeat and realizes the video of me and Aspen on his phone is good for nothing but his spank bank.

Pulling my phone from my pocket, I bring up my messages with Olivia, knowing I need to fill her in about the conversation I just had with her dad. She's a piece of work for sure, but she at least deserves a heads-up to the fact I just blew up our whole fake relationship. I type out a quick message before hitting send.

ME

We need to talk. Meet me after practice? It's important, Liv.

Reaching the locker room, I bypass the lounge, deciding a shower is needed if I'm going to make it through practice *and* a meeting with my ex afterward. Shit is chaotic right now, but on the plus side, things seem to be falling into place. With the weight of my secrets finally falling off my shoulders, I finally feel like I can breathe.

Work flew by. We had four separate emergency visits, two of which required surgery. Doctor Worthington let me be more hands-on than he normally does, which tells me he's beginning to trust me more. He's always been a control freak when it comes to the order of how he wants things done during surgeries, but I get it. If something goes wrong, it's all on him. He's the veterinarian, the most trained medical professional in the building. When he handed me the forceps and told me to move some dog's organs around, I was shocked. I nearly froze in place, but I quickly snapped out of it when I realized I better take him up on his offer before he retracted it.

At the end of the surgery, Doctor Worthington also let me stitch up the outer layers of skin. He hovered over my shoulder the entire time, but I knew what I was doing. I've practiced different stitches thousands of times over the years. It went as smoothly as it possibly could have, and I walked out of surgery feeling on top of the world, like nothing could stop me or bring down my mood.

Until I checked my phone and saw there was still no word from Duke.

I didn't have time to sit around and mope, so after work I headed home and started on my homework after getting a bite to eat. Mountains of schoolwork have been piling up over the weeks while I've been sneaking around with Duke, nonchalantly putting it off and pushing it to the back of my mind. Nothing else has felt like it mattered, but today was a reminder that life goes on outside of Duke. I have huge goals I aim to achieve, and nothing will stand in my way.

I *will* be a veterinarian with my own private clinic someday. I just have to get there.

No man, inconvenience, or hurdle will stop me, especially not Duke.

I pull out my animal science textbook and flip it open to the page I have bookmarked. Flipping through the pages, I realize I have seventy-four pages to read tonight in addition to all of the other work I've let sit for too long. Pushing Duke to the back of my mind, I dive into the book, studying page after page until I lose track of time. I learn all about the psychology of dogs and why they behave the way they do. A lot of it feels like a recap after a decade of self-research, but it's always good to polish up. I did learn that petting a dog for fifteen minutes can lower blood pressure by ten percent.

After animal psychology homework, I move on to zoology, which I don't love as much, but it does intrigue me. I work late into the night, taking in as much information as I can while I'm feeling motivated. Sometime after midnight, I fall asleep in bed with several thick textbooks open beside me.

I didn't hear from Duke today, so I don't know what that means for us. Why would he ghost me after last night?

Chapter Seventeen

DUKE

It's nearly 8 p.m. and Liv is, as usual, late for our meeting. Johnny's is pretty dead tonight, not surprisingly. It's a weeknight and there's no Makos game, so it's business as usual. Last weekend's NHL highlights replay on the flatscreens behind the bar with each of the team's rankings rolling by along the bottom and of course, the Makos are ranking as one of the top teams of the season. As usual.

"Another one?" Johnny asks from the other side of the bar. I check my watch, growing more annoyed with each minute Liv makes me wait.

"Yeah, sure," I reply. Leaning my elbows on the bar, I prepare myself for the conversation I'm about to have. Truthfully, I have no idea what to expect from Olivia. She's a hot head, but she's known for a long time we were never going to last, even if she didn't want to admit it to herself. If anything, me telling Coach myself saved her a *really* awkward conversation.

The bell on the door rings behind me, signaling someone coming or going. Johnny places another beer on the bar in front of me. Pulling out my wallet, I toss a ten on the bar and thank him.

"Okay, I'm here. What was so important I had to miss pilates?" Liv huffs as she pulls out the stool next to me and sits down. "Johnny, can I get a margarita? Extra dry."

"Sure thing, Olivia," Johnny smiles, offering her a gentle nod. Keeping my eyes focused on the TV above the bar, I bring my beer to my lips and take a swig. I have no idea how this conversation is going to go, but I know it needs to happen.

Lowering my beer back to the bar, I clear my throat. "We're done, Liv."

"Ha, you feel like being funny tonight. That's cute, Duke," she laughs. Turning in my chair, I bring my eyes to her, finding her fixing her makeup in her small compact Dior mirror. "I don't have time for this. Can we please get on with whatever was so important that you called for this random and unscheduled meeting?"

A laugh erupts through me. "I said we're done. Done, done. The jig is up. Your dad knows the truth. He knows we're done, that we've *been* done."

She freezes, her eyes slowly moving from the mirror to mine. "Duke, what did you do?" she stutters.

We spend the next hour talking. I tell Olivia everything. About Carter, about Aspen, and surprisingly, the conversation goes better than I expected, aside from her slapping me for telling her dad without her. Which I have to admit, I expected.

"So it's all done, then? And Daddy is okay with it?"

"Yeah, seems to be. Listen, I know we've had our differences, Liv, but I need you to know, I wouldn't have done what I did, the way I did, if I had any other choice."

"You really like this girl, don't you?" she smiles with an unexpected twinkle in her eye, lifting her glass to her lips. My eyes roll in anticipation for some smart-ass comment toward Aspen about how she's not on my "level." But for once, Olivia surprises me. "Good. Happiness looks good on you, Duke. She's a lucky girl, I hope she knows that. And thank you for not letting my mistakes affect our friendship. I know I fucked up, and I just- I hope you know I never meant to hurt you."

"I know, and it's all good. Shit was meant to happen, honestly. I've come to terms with that and I forgave you a long time ago," I admit.

It's true. Even after the shit that went down with Olivia and I, I still don't think she's a bad person. Sure, she has flaws, *a lot* of them, but in the end, she does genuinely care for those closest to her. Even if she has a weird way of showing it.

She tosses back the last of her drink and pats her lips with a napkin. "I should get going, but this was nice. Thank you, Duke." She makes to pay Johnny for her drink and I stop her.

"This one is on me, enjoy the rest of your night," I say, tossing Johnny a twenty from my wallet. He takes it and tucks it into the pouch of his apron, offering me a nod of understanding.

"Such a gentleman," Olivia smirks. "Take care of yourself, Lexington." We exchange a friendly hug before she heads out, and I turn my sights back to the NHL highlights on the screen above the bar.

Finally, things are falling into place. Who knew Carter's pathetic attempt at stealing my patch would end up being just what I needed to get my shit together. I still have to handle shit with my parents, but that's the last thing on my mind. Bringing the beer to my lips, I guzzle down the last of it before putting my coat back on. The only thing I want to do now is tell Aspen that Olivia and I are done. I'm done waiting for the world to know she's mine. I'll handle whatever bullshit that brings afterwards.

I see Johnny at the other end of the bar serving up some beers to a couple of older gents and shout, "I'm out, Johnny, have a good night."

"Eh, alright, kid. See ya around," he replies with a

salute before I head back out to the cold snowy streets of downtown New York.

Climbing in my car, I push the start button. The engine roars to life and instantly my blood starts pumping. It's been a day since I saw Aspen and even though she's been messaging me, I haven't responded to her. This fucking kills me, but I didn't want to worry her, and I haven't known what to say to her. I needed to figure shit out before I talked to her.

Pulling out of the lot to head toward Aspen's, I find myself still mindblown how smoothly everything seemed to go. Coach wasn't mad, I didn't lose my spot on the team or my captain's patch, Olivia was just as happy as me that the secret was out, and in some fucked up way, our friendship is better than ever. The best part is that little shit Bishop got fuck all out of his master plan. Won't stop me from showing him what happens to people who fuck around with me and mine, though. And now, Aspen is mine.

My phone vibrates in my pocket, but I ignore it. Whatever it is can wait. Seeing Aspen is the only thing that matters right now.

The streets are slick with freshly fallen snow, and even though it's early evening, the sky is already a deep onyx color. Traffic is horrible, but it always is in New York. I crank the music, and *Promise* by Kid Ink blasts through the speakers as I tap my fingers to the beat on the steering wheel. Adrenaline pumps through me with the anticipation of finally seeing Aspen. Of finally being able to tell her that we don't have to be a secret anymore.

I don't care if it takes me all fucking night to cross the city and get to her.

As I pull up to Aspen's, my phone is still blowing up in my pocket.

"Holy fuck," I sigh, annoyed by the nonstop notifications. Parking, I turn off the ignition and finally slide it out of my pocket to see what the fuss is about. Notifications from the team group chat cover my home screen. Swiping up, I type in my passcode and bring up the chat.

> **MATHERS**
>
> Cap? What the fuck is going on?
>
> **STANLEY**
>
> Bishop, what the fuck did you do, man? It's gone viral. I just got a text from Myers, he said Ace is losing his shit.
>
> **RICE**
>
> Yo, props, Duke. She's a dime.

Fury builds within me as my phone continues to vibrate in my hand. The guys are blowing up the chat with questions and comments. Some are pissed. They think I'm fucking the enemy, while others are congratulating me. Those closest to me are concerned, but it's not me they should be concerned about.

Bishop sent out the video of Aspen and me when he didn't get what he wanted. He didn't care that I tried to give it to him. He didn't care that Aspen would be the only one hurt by it at this point.

"That motherfucker," I growl. I inhale deeply, calming myself before typing into the chat.

ME

You're a dead man, Bishop.

Bishop

Bring it. We both know you ain't going to do shit. I gave you a chance, should've given me what I wanted, Duke.

ME

That's what you think. Turn in your jersey and watch your back. It's a feeding frenzy out there, and us Makos, we're hungry.

Bishop

You can't kick me off the team LOL, you ain't shit.

ME

You're right. But when I'm done with you, you won't be able to skate.

I've been scared before, but nothing to this level. I did everything I could to try and avoid this happening. For her, for *us*. But it wasn't enough, and now I don't know what to do. The winter wind blows through the street, whistling as it whips around my parked car. It's the only sound in the silence that is keeping me from drowning in my own thoughts.

I thought tonight was going to be a good night. I thought for once, that everything was happening how it was meant to and that Aspen and I could spend the night celebrating with each other.

There's no way she's going to want to see me tonight. I can't go in there now. She'll be traumatized, and I already know she won't listen to anything I try to say to her. It's best if I head home for the night and then come back tomorrow to try to explain the situation.

All I can do is hope she'll hear me out.

Chapter Eighteen

ASPEN

I'm abruptly woken up by Ashley as she bursts through my bedroom door, sprinting toward where I lie in my bed. She looks panicked as she shoves my textbooks to the side, clearing a spot for her to sit next to me.

"What's wrong?" I ask as I sit up, dazed and confused by the rude awakening. "What's going on?"

Ashley groans, visibly frustrated and having a hard time finding words. She looks somewhat terrified, and I'm beginning to panic alongside her.

"What?" I ask again, snapping at her for an answer this time.

"You're not going to like this," she says quietly as she rotates her phone in her hand, catching my eye. "There's a video spreading across social media. Jace just sent it to me. Why didn't you tell me you were fucking Duke?"

Horrified, my eyes widen and I shoot up, sitting straight as I take Ashley's phone from her hand. "What's in the video? Who posted it?" The words roll from my lips but I'm feeling numb, shutting down internally as my eyes meet the screen.

I press play faster than I can stop myself, and the sound of my own moans hits my ear. It's a video of Duke fucking me in the locker room. He's slamming my body up against the lockers, and the video is long enough to clearly show our faces. I'm mortified, cupping my mouth with both hands as tears begin to fall down my cheeks.

I'm embarrassed. Ashamed, really.

This should have never happened, but I was too fucking stupid to think clearly enough to walk away. *I dug this grave. I put myself here.*

Disgust and nausea roll through my stomach as the video ends.

"Who posted this?" I ask Ashley through watery eyes.

"No one knows. The poster is anonymous." Ashley places a gentle hand on my leg, watching me quietly. "What were you doing sneaking around with a guy like that? He has a girlfriend, Aspen, and they seemed happy together."

Shaking my head, I bring my knees up to my chest and

wrap my arms around them tightly. "She's not his girlfriend."

"Yes, she is," Ashley persists. "I see them together all the time and they're constantly posting each other all over social media. Everyone knows they're together. If I had known it was *him* you were fucking around with, I would have stopped you weeks ago. You're better than this, Aspen. What happened?"

Glancing up at her, I meet her concerned look. "They aren't actually together. They're pretending to date for status and career jumps. Olivia benefits from the social media hype of dating one of the hottest hockey players in the region, and Duke benefits because Olivia's dad is his coach. He keeps his seat because her dad thinks they're together. It secures his position in the spotlight while boosting her 'influencer' presence."

Ashley is silent as she mulls over my words. I can almost see the wheels turning in her mind, and I'm anxious as I wait for her response. She's going to hate me for keeping this from her, and I don't blame her. I would hate me too. I know how bad this looks.

"How did you find this out? How did you even get close enough to him to know this information? I thought you weren't into hockey players." Her eyes widen as her mouth drops. "Ace and your dad are going to kill you, Aspen."

Knowing she's right, I swallow before saying, "I

know. I'm not into hockey players, but I met him when we were at the bar one night. I didn't know he was a hockey player and I let him walk me home. We didn't even exchange information, but I ran into him again at the Little League fundraiser. It was blizzarding and I didn't have a ride home, so he was going to take me home, but then you texted me saying the power was out and he took me back to his place instead. I wasn't going to go with him, but he confessed the whole thing to me and I was so wet and cold I couldn't argue with going to his penthouse. One thing led to the next, and we ended up hooking up that night. I tried to walk away, I really did. He was persistent and I couldn't resist the urge to be with him. He consumes every corner of my mind and I've fallen for him harder than I meant to." The words fall from my mouth like vomit, spraying all over the room. Ashley's face is shocked, but she's also smiling.

"I didn't think you had it in you to be so rebellious," she laughs. "I'm actually kind of proud of you."

I scoff, "*Proud* of me? You should be disgusted with me. I snuck around behind everyone's backs for the entire hockey season, lying to everyone just to get some alone time with him." Tucking my face into my hands, I groan. "I haven't heard from him for two days. There's no way he isn't the one who posted the video. Even if it wasn't him, he had to know. Why else would he have ghosted me so suddenly? I should have seen this coming. I feel so fucking stupid."

"You're not stupid." Ashley tsks as she shakes her head. "You were falling for him and he used you. His feelings for you were as fake as his relationship with Olivia. He's the one who should be feeling like shit right now."

"Ace is going to throw the biggest fit," I sigh, reaching for my phone.

I'm not surprised to find my phone has blown up since I fell asleep last night. Forty-eight texts from my brother and dad in a group chat and over a dozen missed calls from them.

I'm so fucking dead.

I'll never live this down. They'll never let me out of their sight again.

'My heart feels broken, bleeding out from inside my chest as I set my phone down. I've disappointed my family, myself, and probably my best friend, but she won't admit it.

He knows the championship will likely come down to the Knights and the Makos, and what better way to fuck with the captain of the rival team? Fuck his little sister, then leak a sex tape of them at the end of the season. It's the only way to save his ass from losing.

He's a fucking coward.

Chapter Nineteen

DUKE

Bang. Bang. Bang.

My fist slams down on the door to Aspen's house. I can hear the TV on the other side along with movement. I know they're home, yet they won't answer. Aspen hasn't even answered my phone calls or texts. She's pissed, understandably.

"Aspen, please just let me explain," I plead as my fist comes down on the door again. The thin wood door vibrates under my strength, shaking in the cheaply made frame. It's taking everything in me not to burst through the door and make her listen. But I know it won't help. If anything, it will just push her further away.

Fuck, this shit hurts.

I thought being cheated on by Olivia hurt more than any pain I've ever felt.

I was wrong.

Having Aspen shut me out is more painful than anything I've ever experienced.

And it's all because of Carter Bishop. I can't wait to fucking handle him if the guys haven't already. No way am I getting on the ice again with the same jersey as that piece of shit.

It's not happening.

Taking out my phone, I dial Aspen's number again, hoping that this time will be different than the last thirty times I've called her only to be ignored. But it's not.

She forwards it directly to voicemail.

Goddamnit.

I snap, clenching my phone in my hand while my fist comes down on the door again.

"Aspen!" I shout, banging on the door again in one last attempt to get her to answer. Again, my attempt is ignored, and when I try to call her, it goes right to voice-mail. She turned her phone off.

My head falls back and my eyes close as I inhale and exhale slowly in an effort to calm myself. I can't force her to talk to me. All I can do is hope that when she's ready, she will.

Heading back to my car, I'm careful not to slip on the black ice coating the pathway. When I'm inside, I rev up the engine, allowing myself one last glance up to Aspen's window in the hope that she'll hear my car and come out.

But she doesn't. The curtain covering her small window doesn't move. Not even the slightest.

I need a drink, or ten.

Not wanting to run into anyone from the team, I boycott Johnny's and head to a dive bar in downtown Manhattan. It's a place I used to visit a lot after Olivia cheated on me and I needed alone time. It's scummy and full of lots of questionable people, but it's a place I won't be recognized and that's what I need tonight.

The entire drive there I sit in silence. No music, just my thoughts. I'm angry, but mostly I'm scared. I'm scared that Aspen will never let me explain what happened. I'm scared that the moment I finally had her, really had her, I lost her.

I was ready to give up everything for her. I fucking *tried* to. But it wasn't enough for Carter. No, that piece of shit had to go fuck up everything good I had in my life all because he couldn't be me.

Pulling up in front of the small dive bar, I place a couple of coins in the meter before heading inside. The moment I'm through the door, I'm hit with the heavy stench of cigarettes and piss. It's potent enough that most people would probably turn around and leave, but I welcome it tonight, knowing the only thing that's going to help tonight is to drink until all the pain I'm feeling is nonexistent. I need to be *numb*.

I take a seat at the bar just as the bartender makes her

way over to me. She's young, probably younger than me, and covered in thick black and gray tribal tattoos. Her inky black hair is styled up on the top of her head, revealing her ears, which are covered in piercings that match the ones on her nose and lips.

"What's your poison?" she asks with a flirtatious tone as she sizes me up.

"Whiskey, on the rocks," I reply coldly. "And keep them coming,"

She nods and grabs a bottle from under the counter. "Your wish is my command." She places it on the bar in front of me and watches me closely as I toss it back and slam it back down on the thick wooden bar. "Well, someone is thirsty," she adds as she begins to refill it.

"Just do your job, I'm not here to chat," I snap. She cocks her brow, clearly shocked by my bluntness but does as she's told before making her way down the bar to the other customers. My phone vibrates in my pocket as I toss back my second drink.

Slamming the glass down, I nod to the bartender to refill it again as I pull my phone out and unlock it. The team group chat is still going off, but I ignore it, turning instead to my texts in hopes that maybe Aspen has messaged me.

Nothing.

Stanley, however, has messaged me to check-in.

STANLEY

You know you could've told me about
Aspen, bro. I would've had your back.

ME

I know that, but it wasn't just about
me. This is exactly what I was trying
to avoid, and now Aspen won't
fucking talk to me.

STANLEY

Yeah. Now that I know what was
going down, I get it. Shit is popping
off. Everyones worried about
you, man.

ME

Why?

STANLEY

Cause you've gone AWOL. Everyone
is flipping out over the video of you
and Aspen. Some of the guys were
placing bets on who could hit it next.

ME

Oh yeah? Who? I'm going to fucking
kill Bishop.

STANLEY

I got that shit handled, alright? Go get
your girl.

The bartender makes her way over and refills my glass.
I'm thankful for Stanley and the guys. I always knew
they'd have my back. But this is a problem even they can't

fix. Aspen needs to know I was ready to give it all up, for her. I toss back the drink, welcoming the burn from the amber liquid as it glides down my throat.

STANLEY

And don't get shit faced man, we have
a game tomorrow, remember? And we
all need to make it in these playoffs.
Don't fuck around.

My jaw clicks. Unlocking my phone again, I open up my message thread with Aspen.

ME

Aspen, I need you to let me explain.
There are things you don't know.
Please just call me when you're ready.

I close my phone, and slide it back into my pocket. I know she won't message me back. Not tonight at least. Tonight, all I can do is drink away my pain and wait for her to be ready. Even if it takes forever.

Chapter Twenty

ASPEN

I'm four shots deep at Johnny's Sports Bar.

Ashley and Brynne convinced me to meet them here after the game tonight. I didn't go to the game, choosing to stay in and continue catching up on schoolwork, but my friends went. They blew up my phone after the game, begging me to meet them at the bar.

I was reluctant at first, not wanting to chance running into Duke, but then I realized I couldn't let him control my life. I can't pick and choose where I go based on the possibility that I'll run into him. He has *clearly* moved on to bigger and better things, so I said fuck it and joined my friends for an evening of drinking and pretending there isn't a video of me getting fucked going viral.

"Let's dance!" Brynne squeals, pointing toward the dance floor.

Swirling a fifth shot of vodka around in my glass, I watch the crowd of people dancing. Hockey players and puck bunnies are everywhere, grinding against each other as though it's one giant orgy. With the championship so close, the puck bunnies are in full heat and the guys know that. I don't intend on going home with anyone tonight, so it repulses me to think about joining in on the "fun." I'd rather sit here and drink, wallowing in self-pity. The alcohol takes the edge off my mood and I'm almost enjoying myself.

"I don't know," I say to Brynne, still eyeing the dancers. "There might be one too many STDs out there for me."

She rolls her eyes, tugging on my hand as she tries to get me to follow her. Ashley is already out there, smack dab in the middle of the crowd with Jace. "You already fucked one of them. What's one more?"

Shock crosses my face, and I sit straighter in my bar chair. "Brynne!" I warn, nearly laughing as I process her words. "I'm not a puck bunny."

She continues pulling on my hand, slightly off balance after downing a few more shots than myself. "I know, but maybe just for tonight? The season is practically over."

I'm about to tell her no when someone walking into the bar catches my eye. I turn to face the door, and my jaw drops when my vision focuses on a male's face.

It's Duke.

He's with a few of his buddies, laughing and mingling as though we aren't the most shared video across the college hockey leagues. I feel butterflies for a split second, then they're abruptly replaced with disgust and anger.

He did this.

I've been embarrassed and exposed more than I ever thought possible, and it's all because of him. His long game was never to end up with me but to get to the championship one way or another, and I was an easy pawn caught in his path. I was nothing more than a casualty amongst the masses. I made stupid choices along the way, but that doesn't mean I deserve the consequence of being the star of a leaked sex tape. No one deserves that.

We lock eyes as he reaches a table where some of his teammates have been drinking. There's a tired look on his face as he watches me, far different from the look he gave off seconds ago. I watch him swallow hard, resting his hands on the table in front of him. Tears well in my eyes, and I can't look at him any longer.

Downing the shot of vodka, I slam the glass down on the bar top. I don't bat an eye as the liquid slides down the back of my throat, setting fire to my soul. "Let's go," I announce to Brynne as I jump out of my chair, now energized by more liquid courage.

If Duke wants the world to think I'm a slut, I'll show him one.

Instead of letting Brynne lead me across the room, I practically drag her drunk ass out there. The bass of the music thumps against my chest, making me feel alive as we work our way into the middle. Ashley sees us right away and she waves. There's sweat dripping down her body, but she doesn't seem to care. Her hair is plastered to her face as she grinds against Jace. He looks like he's had just as much to drink as her if not more. They're moving as smoothly as their intoxicated bodies will allow, and I let out an amused laugh as I watch them.

There's a Makos player eyeing me from a few feet away, so I sway my hips to the beat as I bite my bottom lip, watching him with the most seductive face I can manage. He smiles when he sees me, nodding his head as he works his way closer to me. Who would be better to take home than one of Duke's teammates? No one.

The Makos player grabs me from behind, gripping my hips as he drives my ass into him. The music slows to a deeper beat, and I begin grinding on him in long, drawn-out motions, bending forward and pressing my backside into him as he holds onto me. I give him a show, mastering my newly-found slutty side as I ride out the emotions I'm feeling.

I turn to face him as the song changes, wrapping one arm around his neck while placing the other firmly against his chest. He's smaller than Duke, but he's still well-built and strong with an athletic body. His face isn't the prettiest, but I don't care. He's my best shot at hurting Duke, even if it's just a little.

My new friend slinks his arm around my backside and grips my ass with both hands, shaking it so that it bounces up and down. I moan, throwing my head back as he works my body. The alcohol blurs my vision slightly, but I can see Duke still sitting at the table. His sights are locked on us, and his face is bright red. He looks like he's raging and about to explode. The hands he's resting on top of the table are turning bright white as he clenches them, rolling his thumb inside his fist.

Smiling at what I've done, I grab the player's chin, bringing his face down to mine. He doesn't resist, meeting my lips with eagerness as I crash into him. His tongue immediately pokes at my mouth, and I grant him entry, allowing him to dominate me. There's a minty flavor to his mouth, making it that much easier to swap spit with someone I've never even spoken to. We haven't exchanged as much as one word.

He backs me out of the crowd, his lips never leaving mine as he pushes us to the back of the bar. My back slams against a brick wall and the player picks me up. I wrap my legs around his torso, and I immediately feel how hard he is. Reaching down, I run my hand over the growing bulge of his jeans. Moaning into my mouth, he jerks his hips, pressing into me harder. I nip at his bottom lip, tangling my fingers through his hair.

His mouth leaves mine to trail wet kisses across my jawline and down my neck. One of his hands is kneading my boob, playing with my nipple over my thin shirt and bralette. I close my eyes, trying to let my arousal take over.

A glass breaks across the bar, causing me to open my eyes. I immediately see Duke stalking across the room. The crowd has stopped dancing and they're moving out of his way as quickly as they can. He's heading straight for us, and the look on his face tells me he's ready to kill his teammate.

"Get the fuck off of her," Duke spits as he grabs the back of the player's shirt, dragging him off of me, straight to the ground, where he doesn't hesitate to begin beating the shit out of him.

Blood sprays at my ankles as Duke smashes his fist into the player's nose, forcing me to jump back. "Duke!" I scream, frantically tugging at his shirt to get him off the player.

My strength is no match against him, and it's like I'm not even there. He's lost in a rage as he pounds the life out of the player. He's not even putting up a fight, too drunk to muster the coordination to hit back.

"You film us fucking, release the video after black-mailing me with it, then you have the audacity to try to fuck her in front of me?" Duke's words are full of hate as he holds the player off the ground by his shirt.

"I don't know what you're talking about," the player spits, spewing blood and a tooth all over his shirt.

The rage in Duke's eyes lights up again, and he draws his fist back in preparation to hit the guy again. "You know exactly what I'm talking about. You wanted my seat *and* my girl, and you were willing to set my life on fire for it. You're a fucking coward, Bishop."

Bishop's eyes drop and I notice the look of defeat on his face. "I'm sorry, man. I don't know what you want me to say."

"I want you to admit what you've done, and stay the fuck away from Aspen. I was willing to give up *everything*, and that wasn't good enough for you. My scholarship, my career. Fucking everything, man. You were supposed to be my teammate, not my biggest enemy." Duke lets go of Bishop, letting his drunk body sink to the floor.

Glancing up at me, Bishop says, "I'm sorry."

My jaw drops and my lips part as I gasp, looking between Duke and Bishop.

It can't be true.

It wasn't Duke? He wasn't trying to hurt me? He was willing to give up hockey and his scholarships for me. The NHL? My heart sinks into my stomach, realizing I've been angry at the wrong person.

Duke turns and scans my body, clearly looking for any

sign of injury. "I'm sorry," he mutters when all he finds is Bishop's blood on my ankles.

I'm speechless as Duke begins walking away. The entire bar is silent, watching the event unfold as though we're their new favorite reality TV series. I look around, taking in each of their faces. Even my friends are standing there, motionless and in awe as they observe the chaos.

Duke is a few feet away when I snap out of it. I leave Bishop bleeding at my feet and race to Duke, taking his hand in mine before dragging him out of the bar. He doesn't resist as I lead him to the alleyway out back.

"You were going to give up everything for me?" I ask, tears welling in my waterline.

He's still out of breath, and there are hundreds of blood droplets plastered across his face, but he looks more sexy than ever. He's amped up, testosterone flowing through his body, and suddenly *I'm* the one who feels like a puck bunny in heat.

He nods, confirming my words. "Everything."

Wrapping my arms around his neck, I pull him to me at the same time as he lifts me off the ground, pressing me up against the building behind us. I can feel the music in the bar as it begins playing once more, vibrating through the wall and into my back. Our lips collide, moving in perfect unison as we take each other in, desperately craving more.

Duke raises my dress over my hips, then unbuckles

and unbuttons his jeans, freeing his dick. It presses against me, but it's stopped by my lace panties. Duke uses a finger to swipe them to the side, then dips it inside me. He pumps a finger inside me two or three times before inserting a second finger, coating it in my arousal.

Nobody makes me as wet as Duke Lexington. He drives me absolutely insane in the best way possible.

His thumb rubs over my clit while he works my pussy, stretching me in preparation for his cock. My head falls back as I let out a moan, crying out into the alleyway for more of him.

"I need you to fuck me," I beg, grinding up against his fingers as I seek more girth.

Duke smirks, letting out a light chuckle. "I'm getting to it." He withdraws his fingers from me, then grips his dick, lining it up against my entrance. "I'm going to fuck you tonight, and every night, and I don't care who knows. You are *mine,* Aspen Anderson. No one else's. Your body belongs to me."

His words spark something deep inside me, igniting a fire as I process them. He *does* want me. He was willing to give it all up for me.

I don't care what Ace or my dad want. *This is what I want, what I need.*

I'm right where I'm supposed to be.

Duke presses into me, working his way inch by inch until he's fully inside of me. He slides out, then thrusts back in with enough force to nearly knock the wind out of me. I cry out, digging my nails into his back as he begins pounding into me, fucking me as fast and hard as he can. His breath quickens, and he's breathing harder with each stroke. My moans can probably be heard from down the street, but I don't care.

I don't care what anyone has to say.

Duke Lexington is mine.

His hands are holding me so firmly that it almost hurts, but it drives my adrenaline higher. Using his shoulders as support, I match his pace, bouncing up and down on his dick. He's slamming in and out of me so quickly I can't breathe, and I'm going to explode instead.

"Duke!" I scream, coming all over his dick as I reach my climax. My core tightens and my toes curl as he draws out my orgasm, pounding me like our lives depend on it.

Seconds later he follows, spilling himself inside of me as I come down from the high.

I sigh, closing my eyes as I rest my head against his chest. We're both breathing hard and I can feel his heart racing.

He's mine.

Chapter Twenty-One

DUKE

Stepping off the elevator and into my penthouse with Aspen on my arm feels fucking phenomenal. I have to admit, for a bit there, I thought the shit Bishop pulled was going to cost me her, and I was ready to let her go if that was what she truly wanted. But the moment I saw him make a move on her, that darkness in me snapped. My hands are still aching and swollen from finally giving Bishop the beating he deserved.

"Do you want a drink?" Aspen asks as she makes her way across the large open space to my kitchen. She drops her purse on the counter and heads to the cupboard where she knows I keep the glasses and pulls out two.

"Yeah, sure," I reply. My hockey bag is lying across one half of the oversized couch with my hockey stick leaned up against it. When I plop down on the couch, the stick falls, making a loud banging sound that echoes around the penthouse as it hits the floor. Too tired to care, I kick off my shoes and watch as my girl makes herself at home in my kitchen. Fuck if that doesn't do some shit to my insides. My lips pull into a smile and as if sensing my eyes on her, she lifts hers to mine and laughs.

"Can I help you with something?" she teases cockily as she fills her glass with red wine.

"I mean, I can *definitely* come up with a few things you could help me with," I reply.

"It's been less than ten minutes since I *helped* you. Do you really mean to tell me you need more, already?"

"Baby, I'll never tire of you helping me with that," I smirk coyly as she makes her way over. Aspen hands me the glass of amber whiskey as she climbs on my lap.

"Is that so?" she asks. Reaching up, I tuck one of her loose curls behind her ear before cupping her face with my hand. My thumb softly brushes over her plump lip.

"It is," I reply as my eyes follow my thumb's movement. Aspen catches me off guard, gently taking my thumb between her teeth. A growl builds in my chest, and my cock hardens. "Aspen..." I whisper.

"Duke," she taunts, her voice barely audible as she wraps her lips around my thumb and sucks. My cock springs to life, craving her mouth's warmth and softness wrapped around it.

"Are you trying to get fucked right here, right now?" I

question, pulling my thumb from her lips. She smiles, biting her bottom lip.

"I mean, I'm trying to play. You like to play, don't you, Duke?" she asks innocently. Taking my glass and hers, she places them on the small coffee table in front of us. "After all, the big game is tomorrow. Maybe a night of fucking will bring you good luck."

Tomorrow's championship game is against her brother's team. Knowing my girl is cheering me on even though I'm facing off against her brother and dad means a lot to me. But I'm also concerned about how they're going to react after seeing the video and finding out about me and Aspen. I know for a fact that Ace won't approve, but I'd be lying if I said I wasn't at least a little excited to piss him off.

I force the thoughts of tomorrow's problems from my head. Tonight is about Aspen and me. No one else.

"You know, I think you're right," I whisper against the shell of her ear before sliding myself out from under her.

Confused, she re-adjusts herself on the couch as I lower myself to the floor and kneel in front of her. Keeping my eyes locked with hers, I teasingly run my hands up and down her thighs overtop her thin black leggings. Her body melts into my touch, and from the look in her eyes, I can see she's enjoying it, even if she's unsure of what's happening.

"What's the matter, Aspen? I thought you wanted to

play?" I whisper with a husky tone as I lower my mouth to her knee. I nip and pull at the thin fabric with my teeth, tightening my grip on her hips, holding her in place before running my flattened tongue up her thigh.

"Duke," she whimpers, clearly hungry for more.

With my hands on her hips, I hook my fingers under the waist of her leggings and pull them down slowly. Inch by inch she squirms to help me. With the smooth skin of her upper thighs exposed, I waste no time, peppering soft kisses down them and across the tops of her knees as I guide her pants down her legs. Tossing them to the side, I turn my eyes back to hers. She's leaned back into the couch, wearing nothing more than a pair of thin lace panties and a tank top. Her face is flushed with a light pink shade that she looks fucking gorgeous in. Her hair is fanned out behind her in silvery locks that shine in the dim lights hanging from the high ceiling.

"Fuck, baby. You are easily the most beautiful thing I have ever seen."

And she is. Laying before me like this. Exposed, vulnerable. Right now, Aspen Anderson is splayed out before me like a goddamn goddess, and I'm on my knees worshipping her, begging for the chance to please her. To *taste* her.

The forbidden fruit that is no longer forbidden.

I allow myself a moment to take her in just like this. A moment to take a mental memory of her. She smiles, bringing her finger to her mouth, and she bites down on it shyly under the weight of my stare. I smirk, finding her shyness fucking adorable. I lower myself to her, ghosting my lips over hers again before my tongue glides out and runs across her bottom lip. She moans softly, and as I begin to kiss down her neck and chest, her moans grow louder. Hungrier.

My cock twitches with anticipation. I may have just fucked her in that alley outside of Johnny's but now that she's mine, I need to taste her.

Devour her.

When I reach her panties, I run my tongue across the fabric keeping me from her pussy. She smells like sex. Like me, and fuck if it doesn't send my heart beat into a frenzy. Hooking two fingers under her panties, I pull them to the side before running my tongue across her sensitive flesh. Fuck, she tastes good.

Like honey and whiskey.

Like *mine*.

She twitches and groans. Her hips roll with the movement, and her hands find their way to my still damp hair as she pulls my head into her.

I laugh, "So demanding, and here I thought you wanted to play." She glares down on me, but the moment I flick her swollen clit with my tongue, her eyes roll back, and her head falls into the pillow behind her. My thumb replaces my tongue, rubbing her swollen bud in circular motions as I use my other hand to pin her down by her thigh.

"Oh, fuck, yes."

"Yeah? You like the way my tongue feels, don't you baby?" I ask before sinking my teeth into her inner thigh.

Aspen cries out, her pleasure-filled sounds only making my cock harder and more desperate to bury itself inside her.

"This is my pussy. I got you back, and now it's mine, you hear me?" I whisper against her flesh. I lick and nip at her skin, marking her inner thighs with crimson teeth marks.

"More, Duke," she pleads, clearly as needy for me as I am for her, but not yet. Next to my knee, I can feel my hockey stick still laying on the floor where it fell. Tomorrow's game is the most important game and it will make or break my hockey career going forward, which sparks an idea.

Lifting the stick from the floor, I angle the handle between her thighs. Her eyes widen with panic, but it's brief. My thumb circling her clit increases its speed, making her hips squirm and buck in search of more friction, more *something*. Anything to bring her to the release her body so desperately craves. Still holding her panties to the side, I line the stick up at her opening, swirling its taped handle around in her slick juices.

"Duke, I can't-" she stammers.

"You can, and you will. You're going to fuck my stick like a good fucking girl because I need you to. I need your sweet goddamn juices on my stick when I score the winning goal tomorrow. I want to smell you on my stick when I beat your brother's team and take the championship. Do you understand?"

She nods, though her eyes still reflect a tinge of fear. I spit on her pussy, spreading it around her with the handle before slowly pushing it through her tight entrance.

"Holy fuck," she moans as I watch her pussy swallow my stick.

"That's it, baby. Fuck, look how good your pussy is taking my stick. *Fuck*." My cock is rock hard and throbbing in my pants, begging me to touch it, but I don't. Instead, I slowly move the stick in and out of Aspen, pumping her pussy as she moves to grip the couch behind her, letting her back arch off the cushion. Lowering my head to her thigh, I nip and suck at her flesh while gliding the stick in and out of her. Her hips meet each thrust, welcoming the pleasurable stretch my stick is giving her.

"Duke, please-"

"Please what, baby? Tell me what you need, Aspen," I demand.

"More, harder," she moans. I slide the stick in deeper, harder, filling every inch of her tight pussy with my wood. Her nails are white from how hard she's gripping the couch behind her. Her back is lifted so much it's barely touching the fabric. Her body tenses. She's close.

I continue.

"Cum for me, Aspen. Cum on my fucking stick like a good girl, baby," I whisper.

Resting my chin on her knee, I sink my teeth into her again. Not deep this time, just enough to scratch the surface, sending a chill up her spine and goosebumps to coat her skin, but it's just what she needs. Her body trembles and she cries out with pleasure as her orgasm hits her.

"Oh. My. Fuck. Yes. Oh, Duke."

Once she's ridden out her orgasm, I slowly slide out the stick and toss it back to the floor beside us before running my tongue up and down her pussy, licking and lapping up every drop of her release. She squirms and twitches at the impact of my heated tongue on her sensitive flesh, so I grip her hips and hold her down tightly while I suck up every last drop.

"Don't try to stop me, Aspen. You are mine and that's my fucking cum. I want to taste every bit of you on my tongue."

Looking down at me, her ocean-filled eyes smile. "My turn." Before I know it, she's on the floor with me, pushing the table over to give us more room.

"What are you doing?" I laugh as she pulls at my sweats.

"You said we're playing, but so far, only you've

played. Now, it's my turn." She grins as she slides her hands inside my sweatpants and wraps her tiny hand around my cock. Her other hand pushes me to lay down flat on the floor as she climbs between my legs.

"Is that so?" I ask, finding this little game of hers amusing. Not to mention her shoving me down to have her way with me is fucking hot.

"Shh," she snaps before her tongue runs along my cock from my balls to the tip, eventually wrapping her warm lips around it.

Fuck.

Her head bobs up and down. Taking her hair in my hands, I hold it out of her face while I watch her take me deeper and deeper into her pretty little mouth. Her left hand makes its way to my cock and begins to jerk me off to the motions of her sucking. *Goddamn* does Aspen know how to suck dick. But it's when her free hand finds its way to my balls and begins to massage them that I know I'm done.

"Baby," I warn her. Each jerk of her hand and swish of her tongue brings me seconds closer to filling her pretty little mouth with my cum. "If you don't slow down, I'm not going to last."

"Good," she gives me a cocky grin. "I want to taste you, Duke. I want you to fuck my mouth until you burst, and then I want you to watch me swallow you down, because if I'm yours, you're mine."

Well shit.

Aspen increases the pace of her hand, tightening its grip as it glides up and down my throbbing shaft. Her lips once again wrap around its tip, and she swirls her tongue over and around the head inside her mouth while looking up at me. It does me in.

"Fucking hell."

I explode, filling her mouth with my cum as she takes my cock to the back of her throat. She gags and her eyes tear up, sending black streaks of mascara down her face. But she refuses to ease up. She holds my cock in the back of her throat like a fucking champion as she drinks it down.

When she's done, she wipes her mouth and smiles at me before sticking her tongue out.

"That was a fun game baby, can we play again?"

Laughter erupts through me, "Any fucking time. You're a goddamn champion, babe."

"And tomorrow, you will be too," she adds, softly pressing a kiss to my lips, "which means we should probably get some sleep."

"You're probably right about that," I agree, pushing myself up as I tuck my cock back inside my pants.

"Meet me in the shower?" she winks as she rises to her feet.

"Be there in a minute, babe, just going to clean up."

"Okay," she says as she makes her way down the hall.

I watch her cute little ass bounce as she walks away, and find myself deep in thought about how I was so close to losing her. Thankfully, I have her back and now that I do, I'm not letting anything get between us. Although I'll admit I don't know what to expect tomorrow when I see Ace and her dad at the game.

But one thing is certain, the Makos are leaving it as champions.

Chapter Twenty-Two

ASPEN

My phone won't stop buzzing. Ace and my dad have been calling nonstop since they found out I left the bar with Duke. I ignored them at first, letting it ring, but now I'm sending them straight to voicemail. Each call I decline stresses me out more, but I can't give in to them.

This is what I want. *Duke* is what I want.

They've controlled nearly every aspect of my life for as long as I can remember, and I'm done putting up with it. I'm taking control, and they're going to have to let it happen or leave me the fuck alone. I can't have them constantly hovering over me, asking if I'm making the right decisions and dating the right people.

Who gives a flying fuck if Duke's a hockey player? What difference does it make if it doesn't change the kind of person he is? Duke gives more time and money to his community than anyone else I've ever known.

Who was there to protect me when I actually *needed* it?

Duke.

Not Ace. Not my dad. *Duke.*

I'll wait until after the game to tell them that I'm going to do whatever the fuck I want, and what I want is Duke and for them to find something better to do than harass me for who I'm dating.

At the end of the day, it's none of their business as long as I'm happy, and I've been more happy during this hockey season than I have been in years. Sneaking around with Duke was thrilling, exciting, and pumped life back into my body that was tired of the same routines, but there's more to it than that. Duke means more to me than one season of secrets.

I don't care if they want me to be with him or not. I don't care what they think of this incredibly fucked up situation. It's my life and I'm going to do whatever I want. Not once have I ever tried to control their lives, so why do they feel the need to control mine? Is it because I'm the little sister? The baby of the family?

My phone continues buzzing, and I'm about ready to throw it across the room, but I stop myself at the last second, instead choosing to turn it off and tuck it back into my pocket. I can deal with them later. Right now I need to focus on getting through the day.

It's the Makos versus Knights championship, and I can only imagine what's about to go down on the ice when Ace and Duke meet.

Chapter Twenty-Three

DUKE

Today's the day. The championship game against the Knights. Ace's team.

After the night I spent with Aspen, I'm more than ready for it. Lifting my eyes from my phone, I watch her as she dances around in my kitchen. She's wearing nothing but one of my oversized t-shirts, her panties, and a pair of ankle socks. Her hips sway to the song she's humming as she flips pancakes over my stove. Her thick blonde hair is pulled up into a messy knot bun that bounces around on the top of her head.

If anyone could make chaos look good, it's her.

"Come eat," she demands, pointing the spatula at me.

Pushing myself off the couch, I make my way over to the large island in the middle of the kitchen and take a seat as she places a plate filled with pancakes in front of me.

"This looks great, baby. Thank you."

"Good, eat up. I'm going to go shower and start getting ready." She presses a soft kiss to my cheek.

"Showering without me?" I whine, placing a hand over my heart.

"Well, we both know if I showered with you, neither of us would be washed and ready in time for your game." She winks before turning and making her way down the hall.

She's not wrong.

My lips pull into a smirk as I take my first bite of pancake. *Delicious.* God, she can cook too. I won the fucking lottery. I replay the night before in my head as I eat, and as much as I enjoy every minute of all of it, I find myself concerned about how today will play out. Facing Ace and her dad is going to be hard for her. Defending us to the people closest to her won't be easy. I just hope she knows I have her back.

When I'm done eating, I take my plate to the sink and quickly wash the morning's dishes. Just as I finish up, Aspen makes her way back to the kitchen, her hair still damp as she dries it with a towel. She's wearing my jersey. My number and name are on her back.

I lean back against the counter, raking my eyes across her body. "Makos colors look good on you."

"I think so too," she smiles as she makes her way over

to me. "Personally, I'm growing quite attached to the name stitched across my back."

"Oh yeah?" Wrapping my arms around her, I pull her into me and she giggles as her arms wrap around my neck. "Don't worry about today, okay? I will handle my dad and Ace. You just keep your head in the game, and you bring home that trophy, babe."

Cupping her face, I tilt her chin up to me and softly press my lips against hers. "You have no idea how much it means to me when you tell me to kick your brother's ass."

She grins and brings her hands to rest over mine. "I mean, he's due for a bit of an ass-kicking, and besides, that trophy would look nicer in here than in his room."

I am head over heels for this chick.

IT'S THE THIRD PERIOD. The Makos have been dominating the game so far, to no surprise, but the Knights just scored a lucky shot against Stanley, and he's pissed. With the score tied and the clock running out, shit is getting intense on the ice. It's been easy to avoid Ace and his shit, but now both teams are heated and desperate, meaning I have no choice but to face him . The ice is only so big and I've felt his eyes on me since the first whistle blew.

Standing across from me at center ice, Ace stares at me through his mask as he clamps down aggressively on his mouthguard. I smirk, knowing me being with Aspen has this effect on him.

"I think Anderson's gunning for you, Cap," Rice shouts from my left.

I laugh. "I don't know what he's more mad about, the fact that his baby sis showed up in Makos blue, or that it's *my* name on her back," I reply cockily. I turn my sights to where Aspen sits in the crowd and blow her a kiss that she returns.

"You and my sister are done, Lexington. I'll make sure of it," Ace shouts.

"Will you?" I ask, placing my stick on the ice as the ref readies to drop the puck. "I guess we'll see about that, won't we?" I wink.

"Stay the fuck away from Aspen. She's too good for you."

"Now that I'll agree on, but I have no plans to stay away from her. She wants me, Ace. Accept it."

The puck drops, and I knock it back to Rice, who takes it straight into the Knight's zone.

Ace is hot on my ass, blocking me from helping the guys. Rice passes it to Armstrong, who's made it to the front of the net, but his shot is blocked by the Knight's goalie, and he sends it across the ice back down to the

Makos zone. Ace skates up behind me, checking me into the boards as he makes his way down the ice.

Fucker.

I chase after him and come up behind him, high-sticking him. The end of my stick catches him right under his helmet visor, hitting him in the mouth. His mouth guard falls to the ice and the refs blow the whistle. Stunned, he raises his hand to his mouth before spitting crimson on the ice.

"You motherfucker!" he snaps.

I laugh, "Well, actually, I'm a sister fucker. Tell me, Ace, how's your sister's pussy taste?"

"Fuck you, Lexington," he roars as he skates over to me.

"I mean, I've tasted it too, and *fuck* if she isn't the sweetest thing. She rode my stick all fucking night. It's still coated in her juices," I say as I stand tall before him.

The guys on the ice are circling around us, the refs trying to take control of the situation before shit goes down. But it's no use. I know exactly what I'm doing, and by the way his face is turning red, I know I've won. He drops his gloves, so I drop mine, and then chaos breaks out.

It's Makos versus Knights everywhere on the ice. The crowds are screaming and encouraging the fight. My fist slams into Ace's face and his into my gut. I grab his jersey tightly in my hand, holding him right where I want him as I feed him shot after shot. He wobbles on his skates and his helmet falls to the ice.

I slam my fist into him one more time before the ref yanks me off of him and Ace is pulled back by one of his team members. By the look of him, I definitely broke his nose. A steady stream of blood leaks out and down his jersey as he picks up his gloves and stick and skates off the ice.

"Penalty box for you, Lexington," the ref says as he escorts me off the ice.

"Aw, come on, it was just a bit of fun," I smirk, lifting my eyes to Aspen. She smiles at me and nods before glancing over to where her brother is heading off the ice for medical attention. The ref signals to the announcers a five-minute timer for misconduct and high-sticking and Stanley hands me my gloves and stick.

"Don't worry, Cap. We got this," he assures me before heading back into his net. The glass door closes and the teams take their places in center ice for the puck drop.

Minutes feel like hours as I watch the timer hanging above center ice.

The crowd is screaming and cheering, banging on the glass to hype up the boys and keep them motivated during the power play. It's announced Ace is out for the remainder of the game due to injuries. Good.

We got this.

The Makos have the puck, and they're headed down the ice to the Knights zone. The buzzer sounds, signaling my penalty is over. The end of the power play announcement blasts through the loudspeaker as the ref opens the glass door. The game timer is counting down: less than thirty seconds left of the game.

I head back out on the ice just as Mathers is skating by with the puck. He passes it to me and skates off to get another angle. I stick handle the puck back and forth as I approach the net. The Knights goalie sizes me up, preparing for my shot. Swinging my arm back, I line it up and make him think I'm going to shoot. He falls to the ice to block it, but I don't shoot, instead, I pass it back to Mathers, who passes it to Rice in the front of the net. Swinging his arm back, he takes a shot and sends the puck flying into the net right over the Knights goalie's head.

GOAL.

The crowd erupts in loud cheers. I skate around the back of the Knights net, throwing my stick up in the air, roaring as Rice and Mathers skate into me. Blue and silver confetti falls from the ceiling, coating the ice in Makos colors. The Knights toss their shit around the ice in rage as they face defeat and kiss the win goodbye. Coach and the rest of the team make their way out to the center ice, patting us on the back as photographers and scouts join us in celebrating our win, but there's only one person I want to celebrate with.

My girl.

In the crowd, my eyes find Aspen, cheering and screaming with excitement as she dances around with her friends while wearing my jersey.

My life is fucking perfect.

Chapter Twenty-Four

ASPEN

I ran out onto the ice as soon as I could.

There's sadness in my heart for my brother, so I find him first. When he's done with a quick interview I catch his attention, pulling him into a hug before he can refuse me.

I may be mad at him, but he's my big brother, and I'm always going to be here for him. He's always looked out for me, even if it's been a little too much. I know he means well.

"I'm sorry," I say as I squeeze him. He's sweaty and smells of musk.

"It's fine." His voice is flat, and emotionless as he barely hugs me back. "I'll catch up with you later." Ace goes to pull away, backing out of my hug. I notice him glance down at Duke's jersey as it hangs from my body. There's disgust in his eyes.

My heart hurts a little at the rejection, but I understand his bad mood. He just lost the biggest game of the season, and in addition to that, he's upset at me for everything that's happened. There's pain in his eyes as he turns away, trying to leave the ice.

"I love you," I offer him, gently smiling with a quick wave of my hand.

He gives me some hope when he returns the smile with a weak one of his own, and says, "I love you too, Aspen. I'll text you later."

"Okay," I nod, accepting his need to be alone right now.

He skates off the ice, leaving with the rest of his teammates as they hang their heads low.

People rush by me everywhere, sliding around as they try to celebrate with the Makos. I scan the crowd, looking for my friends and Duke. Ashley and Brynne are right up there with the team, chanting and roaring as they celebrate. Ashley has her arms in the air, reaching out for Jace as he skates toward her. He picks her up off the ice, embracing her in the warmest hug I've ever seen a man give Ashley. It almost makes me wonder if he's *actually* going to stick around and not break her heart.

Brynne is cheering with several other girls, a few of

whom I recognize as people we've gone out with in the past, but no one I'm particularly close with.

Duke and I see each other at the same time, and he immediately skates to me. He scoops me off the ice, and I wrap my legs around him as I pull him into a celebratory kiss. We're both smiling so wide our kiss is mostly teeth, but I don't care.

I'm happy.

Truly, wholly, *happy*.

A deep voice clears beside us, catching our attention. We end our kiss to find my dad standing a few feet away, not wanting to make eye contact while I'm wrapped around Duke. Duke senses this too, so he sets me down gently, only letting go when he knows I'm balanced on the ice.

My dad eyes us for a moment, then looks at Duke and says, "I saw a video of the bar fight, and a few of the guys on the team explained the entire situation."

Duke wraps his hand around the back of his neck, rubbing it as he visibly tenses. "I'm sorry about that," he apologizes.

Holding his hands up, my dad stops him. "There's no need to apologize. Any man willing to give up his future at hockey and get into a fight over my daughter must be good enough to be with her. If that's what she wants," he adds as he turns to me, watching for my expression.

My eyes light up, realizing he's not here to scold either

of us. He's giving us his *approval,* something I thought I'd never receive.

Duke is nearly as speechless as I am, but he manages to form a few words. "Thank you, sir." He holds out his hand for my dad, and my dad takes it, shaking firmly.

"Be good to her, or I really will end your career," he threatens with a half smile.

I'd like to think he's kidding, but I know he's not. My dad will go to great lengths to protect my happiness. Although, sometimes he's the one in the way of it. I'm just overjoyed he's actually moving out of my way and allowing this to happen without a fight.

"I won't let you down," Duke smiles, wrapping one arm around my shoulder.

"I'll let you celebrate," my dad gives us a thumbs up. "I've got a team to lift up."

"Good luck," Duke and I say at the same time. He's going to need it. I know how depressed my brother gets when he loses a game, and this was the biggest one of them all.

My dad nods, then walks away, exiting the ice.

The Makos, their friends, and their families are all that's left on the ice, and it's one big celebration. There's confetti everywhere, still falling from the ceiling as cheers ring out across the rink.

Everyone is smiling, overjoyed by the Makos win.

Ashley and Jace are kissing in the middle of the rink while Brynne is still screaming and yelling with the fans.

I look away from them to find Duke staring down at me, lust and sparkle lighting his eyes. There's a sweet smile spread across his face as he watches me.

"What?" I ask, beaming up at him.

"I'm glad you're here," he says as his lips curve upward. Leaning down, Duke wraps his hand around the back of my neck, using his thumb to stroke my jawline. "You're mine."

Pressing his lips against mine, Duke draws me into a low, passionate kiss. Our lips are one, gliding against each other as we smile.

"I'm yours," I echo his words, gripping his jersey with my fist. "All yours."

Acknowledgments

THANK YOU!!

We are so grateful for our beta readers, editor(Rocky Calvo Edits), our ARC team, our street teams, and our readers. We wouldn't be where we are today without you, and for that we are eternally grateful. Thank you for sticking with us.

Words will never be enough.

Have you joined our Facebook groups?

Dana:

Dark & Dangerous Romance: Dana LeeAnn Reader Group

Melissa:

Dark & Depraved Readers